D0855632

Paul Marchand, F.M.C.

Paul Marchand, F.M.C.

Charles W. Chesnutt

With an introduction by
Matthew Wilson

University Press of Mississippi *Jackson*

Books by Charles W. Chesnutt

Chesnutt, Charles W. *Collected Stories of Charles W. Chesnutt.* Ed. William L. Andrews. New York: Mentor, 1992.

———. *Frederick Douglass.* Boston: Small Maynard, 1899.

———. *Mandy Oxendine.* Ed. Charles Hackenberry. Urbana: U of Illinois P, 1997.

———. *The Colonel's Dream.* 1905. Westport, CT: Greenwood, 1977.

———. *The Conjure Woman and Other Conjure Tales.* Ed. Richard Brodhead. 1899. Durham: Duke UP, 1993.

———. *The House Behind the Cedars.* Ed. Donald B. Gibson. 1900. New York: Penguin, 1993.

———. *The Journals of Charles W. Chesnutt.* Ed. Richard Brodhead. Durham, NC: Duke UP, 1993.

———. *The Marrow of Tradition.* Ed. Eric J. Sundquist. 1901. New York: Penguin, 1993.

———. *The Short Fiction of Charles W. Chesnutt.* Ed. Sylvia Lyons Render. Washington, DC: Howard UP, 1981.

———. *To Be an Author: Letters of Charles W. Chesnutt, 1898–1905.* Eds. Joseph R. McElrath, Jr. and Robert C. Leitz III. Princeton: Princeton UP, 1997.

Manufactured in the United States of America

01 00 99 98 4 3 2 1

The paper in this book meets the guidelines for permanence and durability of the Committee on Production Guidelines for Book Longevity of the Council on Library Resources.

Library of Congress Cataloging-in-Publication Data

Chesnutt, Charles Waddell, 1858–1932.
Paul Marchand, f.m.c. / Charles W. Chesnutt ; with an introduction by Matthew Wilson.
p. cm.
Includes bibliographical references.
ISBN 1-57806-055-9 (cloth : alk. paper)
1. Inheritance and succession—Louisiana—New Orleans—Fiction.
2. Passing (Identity)—Louisiana—New Orleans—Fiction.
3. Intermarriage—Louisiana—New Orleans—Fiction. 4. New Orleans (La.)—Race relations—Fiction. 5. White men—Louisiana—New Orleans—Fiction. I. Title.
PS1292.C6P38 1998
813'.4—dc21 98-24049
CIP

British Library Cataloging-in-Publication Data available

Contents

INTRODUCTION

Paul Marchand, F.M.C. [Free Man of Color], one of Charles W. Chesnutt's six unpublished novels,[1] was written in 1921 after Chesnutt had relinquished his dream of having a career as a writer of fiction, in a period when his writing had become, as William L. Andrews has observed, "increasingly retrospective" (264). Chesnutt tried, unsuccessfully, to interest Houghton Mifflin, Harcourt Brace, and Alfred Knopf in the novel (265), and after their rejections, he apparently put the novel aside, never to return to it.[2] No doubt these publishers saw this novel as little more

[1]In Chesnutt's papers there were a number of unpublished novels. Early in his career he wrote "The Rainbow-Chasers," "Evelyn's Husband," "A Business Career" and *Mandy Oxendine*. In the 1920s, he wrote *Paul Marchand* and "The Quarry."

[2]Although the early manuscript novels were heavily rewritten, Chesnutt did not revise *Paul Marchand* once it had been rejected by these major publishers.

than an anachronism, an imitation of George Washington Cable's New Orleans writings, particularly *Old Creole Days* (1879) and *The Grandissimes* (1880). Like the editors at Small, Maynard and Company, who in 1919 had rejected a volume of Chesnutt's dialect stories entitled *Aunt Hagar's Children,* the editors who read *Paul Marchand, F.M.C.* probably thought that Chesnutt had chosen to work in the "outdated genre" of local color (Andrews 264), one that had not been current for almost a quarter of a century.

Returning retrospectively to the genre of local color in the teens and early twenties, Chesnutt reconnected himself to Cable, Chesnutt's first literary contact and mentor, and he also returned to an imaginative terrain he had explored in one of his first two volumes of short stories, *The Conjure Woman* (1899). In these stories, Chesnutt reimagined the form of the plantation tale, a genre used by white writers to express nostalgia for the antebellum era and "the good old days" of slavery. This genre always employed a white narrator who meets an ex-slave who tells the narrator stories of slavery days. In Chesnutt's hands, however, the genre was inverted, and rather than being an apologia for slavery, it became a subtle and wide-ranging critique of slavery and the racism which sustained it. Significantly, the black storyteller of these tales, Uncle Julius McAdoo, is of mixed racial heritage. The white narrator remarks that McAdoo "was not entirely black," and he had "a slight strain of other than negro blood" (*Collected Stories* 4). McAdoo's mixed-race heritage connects him to the characters in Chesnutt's other 1899 volume, *The Wife of His Youth,* in which he began to explore the lives of mixed-race characters, some of whom are white enough to pass. Chesnutt's imaginative engagement with experiences and dilemmas of mixed-race characters continued throughout his career, and he was still representing their lives in his last two novels, *Paul Marchand* and "The Quarry." This focus on lives that are betwixt and between, caught between whites and blacks, originated in Chesnutt's own experience; he himself was light enough to pass, and for a moment, at seventeen years old, he contemplated that possibility. "I believe I'll leave here [the South] and pass anyhow, for I am as white as any of them," he wrote in his journal (78). He chose, though, not to pass, and in so doing to live within and work against the limitations of the color line in the United States. Characterizing himself as a "voluntary negro" (quoted in Hackenberry xxiv), Chesnutt depicted the liminal experience of mixed-race characters in his two major novels, *The House Behind the Cedars* (1900) and *The Marrow of Tradition* (1901).

In *The House Behind the Cedars*, Chesnutt employed the genre of the tragic mulatta and concentrated on the ultimately futile efforts of Rena Walden to pass as white, but he was also interested in the experience of her brother, John. John's passing over into the white world is so successful that he has married the daughter of a plantation owner and, after the death of his wife and her father, finds himself the sole proprietor of a plantation in the post-Civil War South. His passing, of course, involves wrenching compromises: he must have no contact with his black mother and sister, and he must speak, at all times, like a Southern white man—that is, against the interests of his own family and background. (When he talks, for instance, about current events, whites find him "sound on the subject of negroes" [29].) In Chesnutt's next novel, *The Marrow of Tradition*, his central characters are not interested in passing; rather, they are members of W. E. B. Du Bois's "talented tenth." Dr. Miller has studied "in the hospitals of Paris and Vienna, the two most delightful years of his life" (50), while his wife, Janet, educated in the North to be a schoolteacher, is white enough to pass and is, in all respects, indistinguishable from the middle-class white women around her. Chesnutt places these characters in the Wilmington, North Carolina, riot, or *coup d'état*, during which black office holders and black professionals are driven out of town. Miller's hospital is burned to the ground, and although not driven out himself, he is clearly a test case of the willingness of white Americans to accept a new black professional class. In showing how whites were ideologically committed to refusing black professionals any opportunities, Chesnutt contested Booker T. Washington's widely publicized economic plan. African Americans, Washington said, would not insist on political rights. Instead, individuals would concentrate on producing "what other people wanted and must have," and they would then, Washington argued, "in the same proportion . . . be respected" (142). Chesnutt represented his disagreement with Washington in *The Marrow of Tradition* which leaves its central African American character, Dr. Miller, on the threshold. Asked under extraordinary circumstances to operate on and to try to save the life of a white child, the son of one of the plotters of the *coup d'état*, Miller is told to "come on up. . . . There's time enough, but none to spare" (329).

It is difficult not to read these words in the broader context of white/African American relations at the turn-of-the-century, but five years later the moment already had passed. Chesnutt's final published novel, *The Colonel's Dream* (1905), envisions not even a glimmer of hope. The rich central white character, Colonel French, returns to his Southern home town filled with good intentions and ideas of economic lift only to shipwreck on entrenched racism. The white inhabitants, to preserve the inviolability of the color line, would rather forego the benefits of economic development. When he leaves, the town is in worse shape than when he arrived; collective hopes have been raised and then dashed, and in trying to help individuals, French has only managed to make things worse. Predictably, the novel was not popular in either the North or the South.

Chesnutt's fictions, with the exception of *The Conjure Woman*, were not widely read in his lifetime,[3] and by the time he died in 1932, in the midst of the Harlem Renaissance, he was seen as an anachronism. In recent years, however, his work has been reevaluated, and Eric Sundquist has claimed in *To Wake the Nations* (1993) that Chesnutt ranks "among the major American fiction writers of the nineteenth century" (12). One sign of the high esteem in which Chesnutt is currently held is not only the publication of his novels and stories in widely available paperback editions, but also the recovery of his unpublished and fugitive work—his *Journals* were published in 1993, and his letters and an early manuscript novel, *Mandy Oxendine* (1896-97), were published in 1997. With the publication of *Paul Marchand*, we can see how Chesnutt continued to explore the imaginative terrain that he had marked out as his own in the years after he gave up writing fulltime.

Paul Marchand, F.M.C. is one of Chesnutt's two historical novels (the other is *The Marrow of Tradition*) and his only novel to be set before the Civil War. In it he focuses on Paul Marchand, a rich young quadroon who has been well educated and who has spent several years in France, and on the Creole family of the Beaurepas—the patriarch, Pierre,

[3]For instance, the novel generally considered to be Chesnutt's masterpiece, *The Marrow of Tradition*, sold a meager 3,387 copies in its first two years (*Letters* 172 n.4), while two years later, Thomas Dixon's racist novel, *The Leopard's Spots*, sold over 105,000 copies (*Letters* 172 n.1).

and his five nephews. With one exception these nephews are all degenerate aristocrats, vicious and dissipated like Tom Delamere in *The Marrow of Tradition*. Each of these cousins, again with one exception, publically insults Marchand, but because he is a quadroon, he has no right of redress, and there is no expectation on their part that he has experienced their behavior as insulting. He experiences a capstone insult when he attempts to rescue his sister-in-law from a quadroon ball. Her presence at the ball is tantamount to announcing her sexual availability to white men. If she is discovered when masks are removed, her reputation will be ruined, and Marchand feels that he will not be able to take her to France, as he has planned, and marry her off there. In going to the ball himself, however, Marchand commits a "serious breach of caste." He is discovered, beaten up, and thrown in jail. The next day he is released, under somewhat mysterious circumstances, through the intervention of an important New Orleans lawyer. After the death of Pierre Beaurepas, it is revealed that Marchand is not a quadroon, but white; he is not the son of an unknown white father and black mother, as he had always assumed, but the legitimate son of the head of a major New Orleans family.

The degenerate cousins are appalled but are powerless to contest their uncle's will, and four out of the five are in debt to their uncle's estate. Seemingly accepting his elevation to whiteness and to the leadership of the family, Marchand insists, before he comes to terms with his cousins, that their former insults to him be redressed. Declaring he must defend the family's honor, Marchand meets four of the cousins in duels and wounds three of them in appropriate retribution. After his victory Marchand still has one serious problem: he was married as a quadroon to a quadroon woman, but since he has become a white man, that marriage is null and void.

His wife is suddenly his mistress and his children bastards. In addition, almost as part of the estate, he has been promised in marriage to the beautiful young daughter of an old friend of his father who was, the narrator states, "in the market, for sale to the highest bidder." The women become his moral dilemma, and he decides in the end to renounce his whiteness, to stay faithful to his upbringing, and not to bastardize his children. Although he has renounced the privileges of whiteness, he is uncomfortable living in Louisiana, where he could not, as a white man, be married to the mother of his children: "In a very short time I shall leave New Orleans and move with my family to France, where men are judged by their worth and not by their color, where in all honor my wife can be my wife and my children my children and I need not be ashamed of them nor they afraid of me."

We know almost nothing of the context out of which this novel grew except for a few stray hints from Helen Chesnutt's book on her father. Living in Cleveland, Ohio, Chesnutt realized early in his writing career that the color line was inescapable in literature and that it "runs everywhere so far as the United States is concerned" (*Letters* 171). Although this was a deep and long-term conviction, Chesnutt was surprised when he unwittingly crossed that line. In 1917, he went on vacation with his family, and they toured the Gettysburg battlefield. They were about to be ejected from the restaurant at the Gettysburg Inn when they all began speaking French, apparently convincing the manager and the hostess that they were foreigners and not African Americans. Helen Chesnutt claimed that the family was "very much shocked for they had not had this particular kind of experience before" (274). Nevertheless, Chesnutt certainly knew the all-encompassing quality of the color line, and he also was bitterly aware of the general lack of sympathy and understanding of white Americans. He tellingly wrote to Albion Tourgée in 1893 that "in my intercourse with the best white people of one of the most advanced communities of the United States [Cleveland, Ohio], with whom my business brings me in daily contact, I do not remember but once of hearing the subject of the wrongs of the Negro brought up, except by myself; and when brought up by me, as it has often been, I have observed that it is dismissed as quickly as politeness will permit. They admit that the present situation is all wrong, but they do not regard it as their personal concern, and do not see how they can remedy it" (*Letters* 81). Conditions had worsened by the end of World War I, and despite the work of W. E. B. Du Bois and the NAACP (which Chesnutt was involved in from its founding), few white Americans in the 1920s would have admitted that "the present situation is all wrong."

Chesnutt's daughter was critical of what she perceived to be her father's post–World War I optimism. Her parents, she wrote, thought that "conditions seemed to be improving," but to the Chesnutt children it appeared that "the recognition of the Negro as a human being was rapidly disappearing from American thought" (281). If Chesnutt's daughter's assessment is correct, that might explain his choice in *Paul Marchand* to evade the realities of contemporary America by writing about New Orleans in the first quarter of the nineteenth century. But Chesnutt's choice of a central character—a man who supposes for most of the novel that he has mixed racial ancestry—gives one pause, in particular because of Chesnutt's own ancestry. In fact, one might argue that Chesnutt was making up for an omission he noted years before in the second of his "The Future American" articles in the *Boston Evening Transcript* (25 August 1900, 24). That article, subtitled "A Strain of Dark Blood in the Veins of

Southern Whites," concentrates on examples of racial "amalgamation" and mentions the literary prototypes of amalgamation in Cable and other Southern writers, in particular the beautiful octoroon woman. He goes on to observe that "curiously enough the male octoroon has cut no figure in fiction, except in the case of the melancholy Honoré Grandissime F.M.C.," a character in Cable's novel, *The Grandissimes.* In choosing to make his own male octoroon character better than his white peers, Chesnutt sheds light on his own choice as a young man not to pass, and "to own his color" in William Dean Howells's phrase (701).

Both Chesnutt and his character Marchand can be seen as "voluntary negroes," and both decide to stay loyal to their upbringing and family. This choice is the obverse of that made by John (Walden) Warwick [4] in *The House Behind the Cedars*, and it could also be seen as a validation of the choice Chesnutt made when he was a young man. To pass, (Walden) Warwick remakes himself, but the price of passing is the painful renunciation of family. While (Walden) Warwick is willing to pay that price; Marchand is not. Significantly (Walden) Warwick's family consists of his mother and sister, while Marchand has a wife and children—a wife he would have to renounce and children he would have to bastardize were he to become white. For Marchand, the price is too high, and family continuity, given the history of slavery and the history of octoroon women in New Orleans, becomes of paramount importance to him.

The centrality of family connects Marchand to another of Chesnutt's post-1905 characters, Tom Taylor of Chesnutt's

[4]This character changes his last name from Walden to Warwick when he decides to pass. By using both of his names, I am reminding the reader of his submerged "black" identity.

1912 short story, "The Doll." Confronted by the white man who has killed his father, Taylor, a barber, has the opportunity to slit the murderer's throat but resists the temptation in order to preserve his family: "His own father had died in defense of his daughter; he must live to protect his own" (*Short Fiction* 412). Chestnutt's emphasis on family continuity is clearly seen in the way the conclusion of *Paul Marchand* diverges from that of Mark Twain's 1894 novel, *Pudd'nhead Wilson*. In *Pudd'nhead Wilson*, to keep her infant son from ever being sold, the white slave Roxy switches her baby with the master's (both are blue-eyed and blonde), and so the nominally "black" child grows up as the white master, while the "white" child grows up as a slave. At the end of the novel, when the children are grown, the deception is discovered, and they're switched back. The black character who has been brought up white is sold down river, while the white character, because of his upbringing, is permanently unsuited for life as a white man.

Chesnutt agreed with Twain on environment—one's upbringing, one's socialization is irreversible—but he was without Twain's ambivalence toward heredity. In *Pudd'nhead Wilson* the "black" child brought up as the master's son turns out, of course, to be weak and vicious, a combination that his slave mother, Roxy, blames on his black blood: "It's de nigger in you, dat's what it is. Thirty-one part o' you is white, en on'y one part nigger, en dat po' little one part is yo' *soul*" (109). For Twain, he is evidence of how race mixing leads inevitably to degeneration. By the 1920s Chesnutt had rejected the discourses of blood and constructed a character who does not, when he thinks himself of mixed race, bewail his "fate" or curse "the drop of black blood that 'taints' . . . [his] otherwise pure blood" (*Letters* 66) as do the mixed-race characters of Albion Tourgée. Instead, in rejecting his white patrimony, Marchand says: "My cousin Henri once said, quite truthfully, in my hearing, though the remark was not addressed to me, that blood without breeding cannot make a gentleman. It may be said with equal truth that the race consciousness which is the strongest of the Creole characteristics, is not a matter of blood alone, but in large part the product of education and environment; it is social rather than personal. A man cannot, at my age, change easily his whole outlook upon life, nor can one trained as a quadroon become over night a—Beaurepas," that is, a white man. In choosing to have Marchand remain faithful to his upbringing instead of his "blood," Chesnutt turned on its head one of the tropes of nineteenth-century race fiction, where "white" characters discover, much to their horror, that they are actually "black." In *Paul Marchand, F.M.C.*, a "black" man discovers much to his horror that he is "white."

Marchand's choice, however, to renounce his biological whiteness and the advantages that come with it in favor of his upbringing and his family, is made possible by his wealth, which has come to him from his wife, and by his decision to leave the United States. As William L. Andrews has pointed out, Marchand's move to France recalls the conclusion to Howells's 1892 novel, *An Imperative Duty* (266), but in that novella the main characters live out their lives with an awareness of a "secret" to be hidden. Although physically outside of the United States, they have internalized American race prejudice. Marchand, on the other hand, simply rejects the basis of American racism, and emigrates to France, where he has to hide nothing and where his children will become full French citizens, one of them, ironically, returning to New Orleans as a French military observer during the Civil War. Even in the special circumstances of New Orleans, Marchand feels his liminality, for himself personally and for his family, as an inescapable burden, trapped as he would have been between black and white.

In the scene where he relinquishes his whiteness and his leadership of one of the first families of New Orleans, Marchand says, somewhat mysteriously, to his cousins: "I must confess, gentlemen, that my father's experiment has proved a failure." In what sense might Pierre Beaurepas's treatment of his son be considered an "experiment"? Obviously, it could be seen as an unintended experiment in heredity and environment like Twain's *Pudd'nhead Wilson*, but Marchand's use of this word points back to how Chesnutt has characterized Pierre and to the possibility that what began out of necessity becomes, in Pierre's mind, something entirely different—an experiment, but one with unexpected results.

Early in the novel, Pierre Beaurepas is described as an eighteenth-century rationalist: in his library is a reproduction of Houdon's statue of Voltaire, and Pierre is said to be a "disciple of Rousseau and Voltaire, cynical in his attitude toward life." Seated in his library, Pierre is discovered reading one of the few books named in *Paul Marchand*: "In his hand he held a copy of *Émile*, autographed by the great Jean Jacques himself." *Émile* is Rousseau's extended treatise on education, in which he argues that education is a kind of deformation of the natural man. "Good social institutions are those best fitted to make a man unnatural," he writes (8), and he further argues that eighteenth-century educational practice is like "an intolerable slavery" (50). In contrast, Rousseau proposes a theory of educational benign neglect, where the natural will be cultivated, an educational philosophy that would result in a balance between desire and ability. Rousseau's "fundamental maxim" is "[t]hat man is truly free who desires what he is able to perform, and does what he desires" (56).

Pierre Beaurepas's reading of *Émile* signals that the novel is in some way about the consequences of education, about a "cynical" educational experiment set in a system of racial oppression. This experiment, however, involves not only Paul Marchand but also Pierre's five nephews. Pierre uses an old trusted family slave, Zabet, to set them all up. He instructs her to tell each nephew that she has had a dream of good fortune for him alone, and she urges each to go and visit his uncle. Pierre, a wily businessman, probes them about their affairs, and four out of the five lie to him, making themselves out to be more successful than they really are, but each is happy for a small loan from his uncle. Clearly Pierre is subjecting his nephews to a final test, and all except Philippe are found wanting. Late in the novel there is yet another surprise about Pierre's experiment with his nephews. In going through his father's papers, Marchand discovers a letter to Pierre from the mother of the nephews, a letter in which she refers to her youngest child as "*la petite*," the feminine form of "the little one." Marchand threatens Zabet, who brought the nephews from Haiti to New Orleans, and she reveals that the little girl died in the voyage, and she substituted her own grandson, the son of Pierre's brother and a slave woman. Pierre, then, knew from the time that the five nephews arrive in New Orleans as children that one of them was not "white," and he chose to bring up that child as a white man. When Marchand asks Zabet the name of the child and she whispers it in his ear, the expression on his face which "might very well have masked the joy of anticipated revenge, gave place . . . to an expression very like disappointment." The only reason for him to experience disappointment at this juncture is because the mixed-race nephew is the only decent one, the only one not to insult Marchand—he is disappointed that the racial ringer is Philippe.

Chesnutt has reproduced, in the special circumstances of

Cable's New Orleans with its quadroon class, the basic plot of Twain's *Pudd'nhead Wilson*: a "white" man brought up black, a "black" man brought up white. In both parts of the plot, though, Chestnutt departs from Twain. At the end of Twain's novel, when the truth of ancestry is discovered, each character returns to his "proper" place in the American racist imagination. But the conclusion of Twain's novel is bitter because upbringing has unsuited each man for the place he is forced to occupy. The man brought up white is unprepared for life as a slave, while the man brought up black is completely incapable of being a master. For Chesnutt, on the other hand, the "black" man brought up white turns out to be the most decent and humane of all the nephews, unlike Twain's character who is betrayed, his mother claims, by his black "blood." One is left wondering, then, how to account for Philippe's difference. All the nephews were treated the same—"sent to good schools" and each "upon reaching his majority, was given sufficient money to set himself up in the business of his choice." Despite this scrupulously equal treatment, the pure "white" nephews turn out badly: "when Adolphe Beaurepas entered his uncle's house, the plantation of which he was the nominal owner was mortgaged to the limit of its security value, with foreclosure imminent; . . . Raoul Beaurepas had used the funds of his firm for his own purposes and was threatened with exposure, unless a miracle should happen; . . . the business house of which Hector Beaurepas was the head was on the verge of bankruptcy; [and] . . . Henri Beaurepas owed more debts than he could ever hope to pay out of his income. . . ." Philippe, like his half brothers, "had been bred a gentleman, had been educated, clothed and nurtured as a gentleman, and expected by his own exertions to be able to live as a gentleman." Unlike them, though, "[h]e had no expensive vices—he was neither drunkard, nor gambler, nor roué." The only way the novel gives us to account for the differences among these men who received the same educations and who were given the same opportunities is race—that somehow Philippe is a finer character *because* of the mixture of races he represents.

What Chesnutt does here is to recast imaginatively an idea he had hinted at twenty years before in his articles, "The Future American." In the first of them, he mocked a current "popular theory" that claimed that the "harmonious fusion of the various European elements which now make up our heterogeneous population" would result in a kind of racial "perfection." Somehow, Chesnutt wrote, all of the "undesirable traits" would be eliminated, and the new American would be "as perfect as everything else American" (18 August 1900, 20). In the conclusion to the final article, Chesnutt returned to the idea of improvement, but applied it to racial amalgamation: "The white race is still susceptible of some improvement: and if in time, the more objectionable Negro traits are eliminated, and his better qualities correspondingly developed, his part in the future American race may well be an important and valuable one" (1 September 1900, 24). The racial amalgamation that results in Philippe Beaurepas makes him a finer man than any of his half-brothers, but it does not make him any way a paragon. Although he is decent, he is ultimately not a very "good business man," and under his stewardship "the family fortune . . . sadly dwindled."

If one side of Pierre Beaurepas's experiment proved that the white Beaurepas brothers were evidence of *white* degeneration, while their half-brother is evidence of a successful racial fusion, the other part of the experiment—the education of a white man as a quadroon—turned out to be more complicated and more ambivalent. Confirmed racists, like the cousins, would say in the case of Paul Marchand that environment and training overruled biological whiteness: "He has been bred a quadroon, and blood without breeding is not enough to make a gentleman. . . . He has been trained to subordination, to submission. How could he resent an insult?" When Marchand challenges them for the insults each has given him, they resort to a discourse of blood to explain his behavior. His sense of honor "was a proof . . . of his purity of race. No quadroon could have taken such a course, it was foreign to the quadroon nature." In the racist view, blood trumps environment. What none of them perceives, however, is that their uncle's experiment demonstrates something altogether different—that *education* in large measure determines "nature," for a crucial difference between Marchand and his cousins is that he is brought up in New Orleans but educated in France: "The trust fund . . . had fed and clothed young Marchand, had sent him, when he approached manhood, to school in Paris, where he had spent several happy years, finding, in the free atmosphere of student life in the French capital, the opportunity to expand in mind and spirit. There was no color line in France, nor ever has been, and in that country men of color even at that epoch had occasionally distinguished themselves in war, in art, in letters and in politics." In fact, while in France, Marchand had been "an ardent Republican and had accepted and proclaimed the radical doctrine of *The Rights of Man* as applying to all men, with no reservations." Having lived outside of American racial categories, Marchand is an advocate of equal rights for "all men," quadroons and slaves as well as whites. When he returns to New Orleans, he is compelled to live under a system which deprives him of legal rights and even of the right to his own honor. So Marchand's education has made him a hybrid, someone who can understand the lives of whites, quadroons, and slaves, whereas the education of the cousins enables them to understand nothing but their own narrow experience.

Although his cultural hybridity gives Marchand a wide range of sympathy and understanding, it does not blunt his sense of abiding outrage. What is most upsetting for him in finding out that he is biologically white is that he has become what he hates, and his children bewail the knowledge of his whiteness because "they had . . . heard their father swear a great French oath, that if all the white people of New Orleans had but one neck, and he could hold it in his hands, he would strike it through at a single blow, or wring it like a pullet's. . . . " Refusing to become white, Marchand argues for the paramount importance not only of upbringing but also of education. Though brought up as quadroon, he has been educated as a Frenchman, and if, as Rousseau argues, happiness consists of a sense of proportionateness between "our desires and our powers" (52), then the only place where he can experience that sense of proportionateness is in France. Only outside the system of American racial categorization and oppression can Marchand, in Rousseau's sense, be truly free. One might argue that, in emigrating to France, he is inevitably becoming that thing he hates—a white man—but it is only in the United States where he and his children are seen as "white" or "black." As the concluding paragraphs of the novel make clear, they all escape the trap of whiteness by becoming French.

Although William L. Andrews calls Chesnutt's writing in this period "retrospective," Chesnutt used New Orleans as a plausible setting for his startling experiment in upbringing and education. The novel is also a simultaneous homage to and critique of George Washington Cable. Clearly Chesnutt was drawn to Cable in the late 1890s because Cable's was almost the only white voice raised in protest against the post-Reconstruction treatment of African Americans (and in the second decade of this century Chesnutt may well have also seen the collapse of Cable's career as mirroring his own). In a series of essays written from 1885 to 1888, Cable tried to argue on behalf of the rights of African Americans with a rationality that would have surely appealed to Chesnutt who "retained an eighteenth-century vision of a morally principled world" (Thomas 160). For instance, Cable argued that race prejudice is "caste" prejudice, "not the embodiment of a modern European idea, but the resuscitation of an ancient Asiatic one" (135). At the beginning of his career, "caste" gave Chesnutt a way to conceptualize race as a social construct, [5] but he also saw, more clearly than Cable himself, how Cable was still implicated in the very racism he was attempting to critique. For instance, Cable simply accepted that blacks were "an inferior race" (126) (although he did question the permanence of that inferiority), and he also asserted that the importation of Africans into America "grafted into the citizenship of one of the most intelligent nations in the world six millions of people from one of the most debased nations on the globe" (52). The consequences of this presumed debasement in Cable's fiction is the "melancholy Honoré Grandissime, F.M.C." who, out of a paralysis of the will, his presumed heritage as a man of mixed race, eventually commits suicide.

In the case of *Paul Marchand, F.M.C.* I would like to argue, though, that Chesnutt used New Orleans strategically as the only place in the antebellum period known for its class of persons, the quadroons, between whites and blacks, a class that Chesnutt himself lived in and wrote about for much of

[5]Chesnutt uses the word "caste" eighteen times in *Paul Marchand.*

his career. Paul Marchand is a member of this class by reason of his supposed birth, but also by virtue of his wealth, education, and sophistication. Chesnutt himself recognized his own liminal status early in his life when he wrote in his journal in 1881 that "I am neither fish[,] flesh, nor fowl—neither 'nigger,' poor white, nor 'buckrah.' Too 'stuck up' for the colored folks, and, of course, not recognized by the whites" (157–58). Not only was Chesnutt white enough to pass, but his education estranged him from "colored folks," and he could find, in North Carolina in 1881, no intellectual companionship with whites. Chesnutt's isolation from both groups must have been very difficult; he chronicled how he was "cut off from all intercourse with cultivated society, and from almost every source of improvement" (142). On the other hand, the young Chesnutt characterized the "uneducated" black folk among whom he lived as "the most bigoted, superstitious, hardest headed people in the world!" (81). Years later, Chesnutt gave Dr. Miller in *The Marrow of Tradition* many of the same feelings on a train ride in the "colored" car: "They were noisy, loquacious, happy, dirty, and malodorous . . . and apart from the mere matter of racial sympathy, these people were just as offensive to him as to the whites in the other end of the train" (60–61).

In marking off the space in between blacks and whites as his unique imaginative terrain, Chesnutt was being a good realist, following Henry James's advice: "Write from experience and from experience only" (389). As a realist, Chesnutt was aware of the obstacles he faced in the reception of his work by the white reading public, and he articulated his awareness of some of these obstacles in an 1890 letter to George Washington Cable. Cable had just returned to Chesnutt an early draft of a novel that would eventually become *The House Behind the Cedars*, and he included with the draft a letter from the editor Richard Watson Gilder. Gilder's response to the novel was negative, and Chesnutt's defense of his practice is instructive. Gilder had said that there was something "lacking" in the novel, and Chesnutt wrote that "I dare say the sentiment of the story is a little bit 'amorphous.' It was written under the ever-present consciousness, so hard for me to get rid of, that a very large class of people consider the class the story treats of [characters of mixed-race ancestry] as 'amorphous.' " Chesnutt went on to observe that most representations of African Americans are "blacks, full-blooded, and their chief virtues have been their dog-like fidelity and devotion to their old masters. . . . I don't care to write about these people" (65). A canceled passage in the same letter is even more revealing: "I suspect that my way of looking at these things is 'amorphous' not in the sense of being unnatural but unusual. There are a great many intelligent people who consider the [mulatto] class to which Rena and Wain belong as unnatural" (*Letters* 67, n3). In writing about mixed-race characters, Chesnutt knew that he was trying to row his boat against a current flooding in the other direction. After all, he wrote about these characters at the height of the lynching frenzy and at a moment when he knew, as he recognized in "The Future American" articles, that Americans did not want to admit the extent of racial mixing.

Chesnutt was doing more, though, than just representing aspects of his own experience as a relatively well-to-do, well educated man of mixed-race ancestry. Like other African American writers of this era, he was posing the mixed-race character as a kind of intellectual conundrum. Characters like Rena Walden, John (Walden) Warwick, Janet Miller, and Dr. Miller are indistinguishable in education and behavior from their white counterparts, and three out of the four are also physically indistinguishable. In emphasizing their similarities to white folks of the same class, Chesnutt was pointing out to his audience that the idea "race" is not an essence based on blood, but rather an imaginative construction. This is most clearly illustrated in *The House Behind the Cedars*, when Rena Walden's white finance discovers that she is of mixed-race ancestry. In a blink of an eyelid, his love and adoration turn to "horror" (94), "anger and disgust" (95). She is still the same young woman she was a moment before—her appearance, her education, her behavior are all the same—but she is imaginatively consigned to another order of being, and the characteristics of her presumed essence are read into her. Chestnutt's male mixed-race characters, particularly Dr. Miller, are also indistinguishable from their white peers in attainments and education. (Chesnutt, his daughter reports, received the highest score of any of the candidates the year he took the Ohio Bar Exam [40].)

In the twenty years, however, between *The Marrow of Tradition* and *Paul Marchand*, Chesnutt's use of male mixed-race characters became less nuanced, and in the later novel he created what I think of as a paragon figure, the kind found in earlier novels such as Sutton Griggs's *The Hindered Hand* (1905) and J. McHenry Jones's *Hearts of Gold* (1896). These paragon figures function as counter-arguments to notions of the "natural" inferiority of blacks through their high degree of education, their sophistication, and their wealth of cultural capital. Employing this representative figure, Chesnutt betrayed a nineteenth-century rather than a twentieth-century attitude about African American cultural progress as a sign of innate equality. This attitude can be seen in William Dean Howells's review of Chesnutt's short stories where he listed Chesnutt among other African American exemplars: Frederick Douglass, Booker T. Washington, Paul Lawrence Dunbar, and Henry O. Tanner (701). The all-knowingness and hyper-correctness of paragon figures in Griggs, Jones, and Chesnutt served as a counter-stereotype for a culture which largely believed that mixed-race figures could "*imitate* or parody but not . . . own the property of whiteness" (Sundquist 249). Marchand's largely French education accounts for his qualities as a paragon, but there is a certain aura of unreality about him, particularly when it is revealed that he is one of the best fencers in New Orleans, and when in what is supposed to be a *pro forma* duel he wounds, with supreme ease, three of his cousins.

After the completion of *Paul Marchand, F.M.C.*, Chesnutt continued to find this paragon figure compelling. For instance, he speculated in a 1926 article, "The Negro in Art," that "effective" characters for African American writers might be a Negro millionaire, or a Pullman porter-detective, or a "Negro visionary who would change the world over night and bridge the gap between the races" (quoted in Andrews 267). In 1928 Chesnutt recreated this paragon figure in the setting of the 1920s and reconfigured the central motif of *Paul Marchand, F.M.C.* "The Quarry," Chesnutt's last novel, was based on an incident in Chesnutt's life that was recorded by his daughter. A white man, one Mr. Blank, showed up at Chesnutt's door asking for advice. He and his wife had adopted a child, whom they deeply love, but the child at two years old is beginning to show unmistakable signs of a mixed-race ancestry. Mr. Blank and his wife wanted Chesnutt to help them find an African American family to raise the child because they simply could not take on the burden of raising a black child in 1920s America (Helen Chesnutt 285-87). This incident became the basis for "The Quarry," in which the central figure, the baby given up by his white parents, discovers as an adult that he was "really" white all the time. Making the same decision as Paul Marchand, Donald Glover rejects his biological whiteness in favor of his upbringing, but unlike Marchand, he is engaged in the intellectual struggle against racism. He writes a master's thesis in which he "presented a simple, clear, rational and humane solution" to the race problem. Later, he begins to see, as Chesnutt's male characters are wont to, that his rationality is beside the point when white people's investment in racism is more powerful than their sense of justice. White people, Glover concludes, "found it less irksome and more profitable to label . . . [the race problem] insoluble."

In his last two novels, Chesnutt, played out his fundamental contradictions: Paul Marchand, biologically white, emigrates to France, and his children become French. Donald Glover, biologically white, also stays faithful to his upbringing, but remains in the United States and is engaged in a struggle against racism on a high intellectual plain. In splitting off those contradictions into two separate texts, Chesnutt perhaps inevitably reduced the artistic tension in both. If there is less tension in *Paul Marchand, F.M.C.*, it also may be because of how Chesnutt straddled three centuries: an eighteenth-century rationalist in his intellectual convictions; a late nineteenth-century realist who relied heavily on early nineteenth-century sentimental strategies; and an early twentieth-century social constructionist who anticipated views which gain currency much later in the century. In *Paul Marchand, F.M.C.* we watch Chesnutt struggle artistically with these convictions, and he is, ultimately, unable to resolve them. But on some level, Chesnutt must have known they were unresolvable, and he lived out his life torn between two positions: the conviction that the race problem had reached an impasse and the utopian belief that there was a way out of the impasse.

By the 1920s, the liminality that Marchand found so burdensome had become less of a problem in African American thought because the "mulatto elite," rather than seeing themselves as set apart—between black and white—had begun to identify with the black masses (Williamson 112), an identification that Chesnutt himself, I suspect, never experienced. And although Marchand identifies *culturally* with his upbringing as a man whose ancestry was mixed race, he has no loyalty to any group beyond his immediate family. Like Chesnutt, Marchand at one point "dreamed . . . that he might . . . preach the doctrine of human equality; not offensively, but persuasively, appealing to men's reason and their sense of justice." He learns, however, that racism is not amenable to reason, and his emigration is a rejection of the underlying assumptions of American racism. William L. Andrews calls this rejection "an exercise in wish-fulfillment . . . Chesnutt finally realized in fantasy what would never be actualized in his own lifetime—the liberation of the mixed-blood from the social and psychological prison of racially defined identity" (266). In making this assessment of the novel, Andrews overlooks the fact that Chesnutt offered Marchand another kind of "liberation"—one that he astonishingly refuses. He chooses to identify with his upbringing and to nurture his family, and in having him do so, Chesnutt argues more forcefully than perhaps anywhere else in his writing that race is little more than a social construction, and that one's primary loyalty is to one's family—wife and children—to giving them the best opportunities that life can offer, something that Chesnutt himself clearly did for his own children. It is too easy, though, positioned outside of Chesnutt's dilemmas, to characterize *Paul Marchand, F.M.C.* as an exercise in wish-fulfillment because we must remember that Chesnutt chose not to leave America and chose to stay politically engaged, particularly with the NAACP. What he lost was his career, unlike another African American artist of his generation, the painter Henry O. Tanner, who emigrated to France and who had a long and successful career, but one in which his identity as an African American, at least in his work as an artist, was submerged. Rather than give up the struggle, Chesnutt, unlike Marchand, stubbornly remained in Cleveland and tried, once again, to undermine American racism through fiction.[6]

Throughout his writing, Chesnutt tried to resist America's perennial binary thinking about race: either one is white or black with nothing possible between. Chesnutt represented those of mixed-racial ancestry who have family and cultural ties to both "races" and who feel comfortable identifying with neither. Growing up in mid-nineteenth-century America, however, Chesnutt could be nothing but black in the view of white Americans, and when he realized that he could pass as a white man, he chose, like Paul Marchand, to remain a voluntary negro. That identification with African Americans did not mean that Chesnutt believed that mixed-race Americans should be forced to deny their white ancestry. He saw that move as an oversimplification of our complex history, as well as a kind of denial of family history. Just as John (Walden) Warwick had to deny his black family, so too

[6] In a canceled passage in the 1890 letter to George Washington Cable, Chesnutt wrote that if "I should remain idle for two weeks, at the end of that time I should be ready to close out my affairs and move my family to Europe" (*Letters* 68, n5). In 1887 a Judge Williamson, with whom Chesnutt had been reading law, offered to loan him the money to enable him to emigrate to Europe. Chesnutt refused, his daughter concluded, because he was "an idealist. . . . He felt that success in his own country against terrific odds would be worth more than success in a foreign country" (41).

were mixed race Americans denied connection to their white forebears. Janet Miller, in *The Marrow of Tradition*, is the best example in Chesnutt's work of this dilemma: living in town with a white half-sister whom she strikingly resembles, she had longed all her life to be recognized by that half-sister, but she wanted the recognition to be "freely given from an open heart" with "frank kindliness and sisterly love" (328). When recognition arrives, it is coerced, forced by circumstances, and Janet rejects her sister and chooses to cut herself from her white relatives because her sister's husband has been a primary conspirator in the *coup d'état* during which Janet's son has been killed.

Chesnutt, like all important artists, enlarges our vision. He insisted that the experiences of mixed-race people break us out of the trap of the American racial binary, and that to ignore those experiences is a damaging oversimplication of our collective history. In fact the recent debate about adding a "mixed-race" category to the United States Census demonstrates our continuing confusions about race as we try to think through questions such as the constructedness of "race," the meaning of "blackness" as a sign in our country, and the choices we have in saying who and what we are. In the years prior to 1997 people of mixed-race ancestry had been publically advocating adding the category of mixed race to the census as a way of escaping the binary choices of either black or white. As the debate over this proposal developed, many African Americans worried about the dilution of black political power, while others worried about the potential divisiveness of a racial category very like that of "Colored" in South Africa under the apartheid regime. Toward the end of 1997, the Office of Management and Budget announced that it had rejected a mixed-race category, but it would allow persons on the 2000 census to check off more than one racial category. However, there is a catch: anyone who checks off black as one of his or her racial categories will automatically be counted as black ("Rejection of Multiracial Census Category" 23A). So as far as the United States government is concerned, the "one-drop-of-black-blood" rule still applies.

Chesnutt would have been appalled. In Paul Marchand he identified this particularly American kind of thinking as a "legal fiction," and by this "habit of thought that was to last for generations to come, a man was black for all social purposes, so long as he acknowledged or was known to carry in his veins a drop of black blood." Earlier in his career, in "The Future American" articles, Chesnutt called this "a social fiction" (1 September 1900, 24), and we find ourselves, seventy years after Chesnutt wrote *Paul Marchand*, still caught up in a binary system of racial classification, a system that is a "fiction," a construct. In this novel, Chesnutt used the genres of local color and historical fiction to ask questions that are still with us: once "race" is rejected as a biological category, then it inevitably becomes a term to describe our felt sense of upbringing and family allegiance. Our identities are not, Chesnutt would argue, an essence, nor are they a product of "blood," but of experience, and the imaginative register of that experience has to be broad enough, given our complicated collective history, to recognize those in between and not to force them to shut off one side or other of their history and ancestry. And although Paul Marchand leaves the United States, he is, in his counter-emigration, being a good American—moving to where his family can have the greatest opportunities, a utopian space outside of American racism.

The publication of *Paul Marchand, F.M.C.* would not have been possible without the support of several grants. I would like to thank the Institute for the Arts and Humanistic Studies of Pennsylvania State University and the Capital College Research Council of Penn State Harrisburg for their support of this project. In particular, I would like to thank William J. Mahar, director of the School of Humanities, and Howard Sachs, dean of Research and Graduate Studies for their encouragement. Andrea Wilkinson did excellent work in comparing the word-processed manuscript to the copies of the originals. I would like to offer special thanks to my wife, Marjan van Schaik, who went when she was six months pregnant to Fisk University Library to help resolve textual questions that could not be determined from the copies. Finally, I would like to thank John Slade, Chesnutt's descendent, for permission to publish this novel.

Matthew Wilson
Capital College - Penn State Harrisburg

Works Cited

Andrews, William L. *The Literary Career of Charles W. Chesnutt.* Baton Rouge, Louisiana State UP, 1980.

Cable, George Washington. *The Negro Question: A Selection of Writings on Civil Rights in the South.* Garden City, NY: Doubleday, 1958.

Chesnutt, Charles W. *Collected Stories of Charles W. Chesnutt.* Ed. William L. Andrews. New York: Mentor, 1992.

———. "The Future American: A Complete Race Amalgamation Likely to Occur." *Boston Evening Transcript*, 1 September 1900: 24.

———. "The Future American: A Stream of Dark Blood in the Veins of Southern Whites." *Boston Evening Transcript*, 18 August 1900: 20.

———. "The Future American: A Stream of Dark Blood in the Veins of Southern Whites." *Boston Evening Transcript*, 25 August 1900: 24.

———. *The House Behind the Cedars.* 1900. New York: Penguin, 1993.

———. *The Journals of Charles W. Chesnutt.* Ed. Richard Brodhead. Durham, NC: Duke UP, 1993.

———. *The Marrow of Tradition.* 1901. New York: Penguin, 1993.

———. "The Quarry." Charles W. Chesnutt Papers, Special Collections, Fisk U Library.

———. *The Short Fiction of Charles W. Chesnutt.* Ed. Sylvia Lyons Render. Washington, DC: Howard UP, 1981.

———. *To Be an Author: Letters of Charles W. Chesnutt, 1898–1905.* Eds. Joseph R. McElrath, Jr. and Robert C. Leitz III. Princeton: Princeton UP, 1997.

Chesnutt, Helen. *Charles Waddell Chesnutt: Pioneer of the Color Line.* Chapel Hill, NC: U of North Carolina P, 1952.

Hackenberry, Charles. Introduction. *Mandy Oxendine.* By Charles W. Chesnutt. Urbana: U of Illinois P, 1997. xi–xxviii.

Howells, William Dean."Mr. Charles W. Chesnutt's Stories." *Atlantic Monthly* 85 (1900): 699–701.

James, Henry. *Partial Portraits.* 1888. Ann Arbor: U of Michigan P, 1970.

"Rejection of Multiracial Census Category Divisive." *USA Today*, 3 November 1997: 23A.

Rousseau, Jean-Jacques. *Émile.* Trans. Barbara Forley. London: Dent, 1993.

Sundquist, Eric. *To Wake the Nations: Race in the Making of American Literature.* Cambridge, MA: Harvard UP, 1993.

Thomas, Brook. *American Literary Realism and the Failed Promise of Contract.* Berkeley: U of California P, 1997.

Twain, Mark. *Pudd'nhead Wilson.* 1894. New York: Signet, 1964.

Washington, Booker T. *Up From Slavery.* 1901. New York: Bantam, 1970.

Williamson, Joel. *New People: Miscegenation and Mulattoes in the United States.* New York: Free P, 1980.

FOREWORD

The visit of a French duke to New Orleans, in the early part of the last century, and the social festivities in his honor, are historical incidents. If there was not a Paul Marchand case in New Orleans, there might well have been, for all the elements of such a drama were present, as is clearly set out in the careful studies of life in the old Creole city, by Miss Grace King and Mr. George W. Cable, which are available for the student or the general reader—the author has made free reference to them—as well as in the more obscure records and chronicles from which they drew their information. Had there been such a case, it is conceivable that the principal character might, under the same conditions, have acted as did the Marchand of the story.

The quadroon caste vanished with slavery, in which it had its origin. Indeed long before the Civil War it had begun to decline. Even the memory of it is unknown to the present generation, and it is of no interest except to the romancer or the historian, or to the student of sociology, who may discover some interesting parallels between social conditions in that earlier generation and those in our own. Quadroons and octoroons there are in plenty in the New Orleans of today, as any one with a discriminating eye, taking a walk along Canal Street, may plainly see; but as a distinct class they no longer exist. Since all colored people enjoy the same degree of freedom, and are subject to the same restrictions, there are no longer any legal or social distinctions between the descendants of the former free people of color and those of the former slaves. Social decree has made them all Negroes, no doubt to the advancement of democracy among themselves, perhaps to the betterment of the public morals, but certainly at the expense of accuracy and the picturesque.

But the Father of Waters recks not of such trifles and still pursues his stately course beside the Crescent City. The language of Bienville and its local variant are still heard. The roses still riot in the gardens and on the latticed galleries. The old Creole families still cherish their pride of race and their family traditions, and their ladies still retain an enviable reputation for beauty and for charm—to say nothing of their chicken gumbo.

C.W.C.

Paul Marchand, F.M.C.

I.

In the Vieux Carré

Toward the end of the first quarter of the nineteenth century, New Orleans, the little city planted on the banks of the Mississippi, was in the full tide of a new-born prosperity. Always French at heart, in spite of the successive strains of alien humanity which penetrated and mingled with its population—Spanish, Indian, African, English, Irish, American—it had been nearly a score of years under the government of the United States. Eight or ten years before, General Jackson, defeating the British in a famous battle, had firmly established the American influence, and made the word "Yankee" a symbol of respect, instead of, as formerly, a term of suspicion and reproach. Prosperity had followed the incorporation of the colony into the Republic. From 1812 to 1821 the population had nearly doubled. The Mississippi swarmed with steamboats, laden with cotton and sugar from the up-river districts, destined for shipment to Europe or the North. The old city walls had been torn down, the moat filled up and converted into boulevards. From a sleepy, slow, but picturesque provincial French town, with a

Spanish veneer, the Crescent City had been swept into the current of American life, and pulsed and throbbed with the energy of the giant young nation of the West.

Nevertheless, these changes were in many respects as yet merely superficial. The great heart of the community,—the thoughts, the feelings, the customs, the prejudices, the religion of the people,—remained substantially unchanged. The current was swifter, but the water was the same. The Americans, while tolerated socially, were still a class apart, though by virtue of their superior energy and genius for politics they were rapidly becoming the ruling class. The Creoles had their own very proud and exclusive society. They had resented the Spanish dominion; they were not yet quite reconciled to the American occupation. They were the professional men and the owners of land and slaves, the *rentiers,* or gentlemen of independent income.

Descending by easy grades, there were the people of color—octoroons, quadroons, mulattoes—many of them small tradesmen, a few of them large merchants or planters, and more than one the inheritor of substantial means from a white father or grandfather—an inferior but not entirely degraded class. A battalion of free colored men, for instance, had served gallantly in the War of 1812, and had won the praise of the commander-in-chief; while the quadroon women were famous for their beauty and their charm, neither of which could have existed without some friendly encouragement. At the basis of all lay the black slaves, whose arduous and unrequited toil, upon the broad, deep-soiled plantations of indigo, rice, cotton and sugar cane, furnished the wherewithal to maintain the wealth and luxury of the capital.

One day in the spring of 1821, about ten o'clock in the morning, an old colored woman entered the *vieux carré*, or old square, with a large basket upon her head, and took up her stand in front of the porch of the *Cabildo*, or *Hotel de Ville*, or City Hall, as it was successively called under the various regimes, the beautiful old Spanish building which still faces the *Place d'Armes*, now Jackson Square. She placed her basket on the pavement, removed the clean white cotton cloth which covered it, and disposed for exhibition the contents, consisting of *pralines*, or little crisp sweet cakes, a popular Creole delicacy. She then pulled out from behind one of the columns of the porch a three-legged wooden stool, hers by right of property or prescription, and took her seat upon it by the basket.

"*Pralines!* fresh and sweet! *Pralines, messieurs! Pralines, mesdames! Pralines, mes enfants!*"

Her mellow voice resounded beneath the arches of the porch, and out over the *Place d'Armes.* The leisurely activities of the city were in full swing. It was about the hour for the courts to open, and, as it was a feast day in Lent, a second service in the Cathedral was to begin shortly. More than one gentleman with a sweet tooth stopped in front of the old woman long enough to purchase one of the crisp cakes, which he munched surreptitiously as he went on. Others dropped a coin into the basket, accepting nothing in return but a bow, a curtsey, or the old woman's voluble thanks. A minor city official, entering the Cabildo, stopped a moment to chaff with the old street vendor. The day was warm, the gentleman was stout, and he had removed his hat, which he held in his hand.

"*Bon jour, Zabet!*" he said, "You grow younger and younger. You do not look a day over a hundred." Zabet's reputed great age was a popular myth.

"*Bon jour, miché* (monsieur). *Voulez vous des pralines?* It is hard to determine your age, *Monsieur l'Interprete,* by looking at you. Did you lose your hair from age or early piety?"

The bystanders laughed, and the interpreter, acknowledging his defeat with a shrug and a grimace, entered the building.

An elderly lawyer, with a dignified and imposing mien, attended by a colored servant carrying a brief-case, drew near. He was absorbed in thought and seemed not to observe the old woman's deferential salute. She respected his mood and did not accost him.

"There, my children," she observed sententiously to the group of loiterers about her, "there goes Miché Jules Renard, the great advocate. He is lawyer for Père Antoine, the rector of the parish, and for the very rich Miché Pierre Beaurepas. It was not from any lack of courtesy or consideration that he did not speak to me, for he is one of my best friends, but because he has business on his mind of such moment that he can think of nothing else."

A judge went by. To him Zabet bowed as deeply as her seated position and her girth would permit. No native of New Orleans respected authority more than old Zabet Philosophe—as she was called—Elizabeth the wise woman. For twenty-odd years a fixture in the *vieux carré*, she had been a public institution, known and respected of all men, since General Jackson, nine years before, in the full tide of his popularity, had publicly shaken hands with her on the steps of the Cathedral, had praised her patriotism, commended the gallantry of the free colored troops, and given Zabet a silver dollar. She had kept the dollar ever since, though often offered for it many times its value. It was a standing joke to try to purchase this souvenir.

The judge nodded to the cake-woman. Zabet gave to her audience details, in Gumbo or Negro French, of the judge's imposing pedigree and the grandeur of his ancestors. When addressing white people she spoke excellent French, having lived the greater part of her life in the houses of the rich and cultured, first in San Domingo, from which she had fled, with her master's children, during the insurrection of 1793, and later in New Orleans, where, in recognition of her loyalty, she had for half a century enjoyed the privileges of a free woman. Indeed, her immunity from slavery had lasted so long that her free papers were never asked for—no more than one would have looked for the charter of the city or the title deeds of the Cabildo. She was old, and fat, and brown as old mahogany; but she had once been young and fair and slender, and her wisdom was that of a varied, not to say variegated experience. She had been by turns seamstress, hairdresser, laundress, nurse and midwife, and had become a seller of cakes only when age and rheumatism had disqualified her somewhat for more active pursuits. She was the repository of more than one family secret, and discretion was one of her few virtues.

Shortly after the judge had disappeared within the doorway of the city hall, a Creole gentleman of about thirty, dressed in the European fashion which the Creoles affected, with very high collar, full shirt front and voluminous cravat, top boots with large flaps, and somewhat stouter of build and less open of countenance than most men of his race, approached old Zabet on the way to the Cabildo. To this gentleman, a member of the family which held the dormant title to the old cake-woman,—she being, though she had forgotten it, a chattel personal,—Zabet Philosophe instinctively yielded the deference due his name, and, rising laboriously from her stool, greeted him with a profound curtsey, to which he responded with an absent-minded nod.

"Miché Adolphe seems depressed," suggested the old woman, insinuatingly.

The appearance of the stout gentleman bore out this

conjecture. He looked decidedly worried. At the old woman's remark he paused in front of her and sighed.

"I had a dream, last night, Miché Adolphe," she said, "in which you had fallen into the river. You had gone down twice, and were throwing up your hands for the last time."

It was a superstitious age, and Zabet's dreams were an easy expedient, by which she was able to talk to white people with a freedom which would not have been permitted to less privileged colored persons.

"You should not presume to dream of me, old witch, unless your dreams are good ones. No need to predict bad luck—it is mine already!"

"But you are too impatient, master! That was not all of my dream. You were rescued at the last moment."

"By whom?" he demanded eagerly.

Zabet Philosophe's dreams had often come true; this had been known to happen many times. The guesses of a shrewd observer who understands the character and circumstances of those about, may often hit the mark. Moreover Zabet's dreams were often shrewdly calculated, as in this instance, to accomplish indirectly some very definite purpose.

"By your uncle Pierre," she rejoined, "who threw you a plank, *mon Dieu,* upon which you swam safely ashore!"

Adolphe Beaurepas's face lit up with hope. Was this dream of the old mulatress a good omen? Was it at all possible that his close-fisted uncle Pierre would help him to lift the miserable mortgage, ripe for foreclosure, which covered the whole of his small estate?

"Tell me, Zabet!" he said, dropping into the Philosophe's basket one of his few pieces of silver, "do you think he would care to see me?"

"He received you affectionately in my dream," returned Zabet, "which was one of the true kind. I saw Miché Pierre only last night, and he spoke of his dear nephews and of how much he loved them. And he added that he was growing old, and must decide upon his heir."

"Dear, good uncle!" replied Adolph Beaurepas, with a cunning smile. "He does not know how much I love him. I think I shall pay him a visit."

"By all means," returned Zabet. "I should not neglect it. Out of sight, out of mind."

"*Merci,* Zabet, I'll go and see him."

"Go in the morning, Miché Adolphe, when he is fresh and his mind clear. You will have a better reception."

The court had not yet opened, but the hour for opening was at hand, and several belated lawyers hurried past with their clients and witnesses. As a gentleman, taller of stature than most Creole men, who as a rule, though athletic, were of about the middle height, passed old Zabet in too great haste to notice her, she called out to him.

"There is no need to hurry, Miché Henri. The judge has not yet gone in. I was at Miché Pierre's house this morning."

"And how is my uncle?" queried Henri Beaurepas, another of the nephews of the rich Creole proprietor referred to by Zabet.

"Failing, Miché Henri, though he does not seem to realize it."

Standing in the glare of the morning sun, Henri Beaurepas's face showed indubitable marks of dissipation. Late hours do not conduce to early rising or firm cheeks or clear eyes. He had sat in a gambling house on Canal Street until three o'clock that morning, and had suffered heavy losses at cards, for which he had given his notes of hand, payable on demand, thus increasing the total of his debts by several thousand dollars. His expression brightened when the old woman spoke.

"Why do you think he is failing, Zabet?" he asked with restrained eagerness.

"Why, Miché Henri? Because he is thinking of his heir. He asked about you. He spoke very kindly. I think he would like to see you."

Another silver piece dropped into the old woman's basket.

"I'll go and see him, Zabet. When is he in the best humor?"

"I should go just before noon, Miché Henri—before luncheon. He is apt then to be in a pleasant mood. But there comes your judge."

"Then I must hurry in, and finish my testimony. I am a witness in the Janvier case. *Merci,* Zabet; when I come into the estate, I'll not forget you." The Janvier case was a famous, long drawn out piece of litigation involving the title to a large tract of valuable land.

"*Merci,* Miché," said Zabet, with a curtsey, but the smile with which she followed the gentleman as he entered the city hall, had more of shrewd cynicism than of the servility which had marked it when face to face with her interlocutor. Among other things which slavery had taught Zabet, if she needed any instruction, was, when she chose, the ability to so control her features that they did not reveal her thoughts, a very valuable accomplishment for one of her condition.

There was a lull in the street movement for a brief space, and then the bells of the Cathedral nearby rang out for morning mass. This venerable and imposing pile, with its mixture of rustic, Tuscan and Roman Doric styles of architecture, its towers lined with low spires, and its arched door with clustered columns on either hand, occupied one side of the old square, and was the recognized center of the Creole life of New Orleans.

As the bells rang out, a shabby one-horse carriage, drawn by a flea-bitten gray gelding, which, in spite of its age, showed signs of breeding, entered the Square from St. Anne Street, and passing old Zabet, who dropped an unnoticed curtsey to the occupants, drew up in front of the Cathedral door. From it dismounted an elderly Spaniard, with the pointed Velasquez beard affected by men of his race. He was followed by a young woman of rare beauty, whom he assisted to alight. They might have been, as they were in fact, father and daughter.

Zabet, who stood not far from the door of the church, with her eyes fixed upon the couple, did not, for the moment, perceive two gentlemen who were approaching her on the street from opposite directions. Each of these, it seemed, was also intent upon the pair in front of the Cathedral, and neither perceived the other until they came into personal contact, though with no great degree of violence, for both were walking slowly, immediately in front of the old cake merchant.

One of the two, a handsome young man, of about the middle height, with a proud expression, tinged with a melancholy discontent, had drawn back deprecatingly, and was lifting his hat with a murmured apology, when the other, with a truculent air, drew back his arm almost involuntarily, and struck the first a stinging blow upon the cheek.

"You should stick to the gutter, *canaille,* if you cannot keep out of the way of gentlemen! If you kept your eyes in front of you, instead of staring insolently at white ladies, it would be the better for you. This is not your first offense. You will need more than one lesson to teach you your place."

The person thus addressed, who was apparently no more responsible for the accident than the speaker, turned white at first,—whether with fear or with anger,—but almost instantly the tide of blood flowed back and flushed his cheek a dark crimson, and from his black eyes blazed the fierce resentment to which the blow had given rise. Such of the bystanders as did not know the two men, held their breath for a moment, in anticipation of the tragedy which would in all probability follow so grievous an insult. The men of New Orleans were hot-blooded and impulsive, prone to act first and think afterwards, if the matter demanded thought. Among the Creole French and Spaniards the point of honor was jealously guarded, and frequent resort was had to the code for its maintenance, while among the American adventurers who came down the Mississippi were many violent men who had sought the city because of its distance from courts where their presence was urgently desired. Only the week before, a prominent citizen had been shot down for a less offense than a blow or running into another, and brawls between commoner men were of frequent occurrence.

To the surprise and disappointment of the bystanders, however, the man who had been struck, after a visible effort to restrain himself, made no reply, but merely turned upon his heel and walked quietly away. Around the next corner, however, in a quiet street where he was out of sight and hearing, he first relieved his mind by a flow of strong language which he muttered under his breath, accompanied by gestures significative of defiance and revenge, and then, after this harmless and somewhat childish though perfectly natural performance, drew from his pocket a set of tablets, glanced at the clock in the cathedral near by, and made a careful memorandum with the gold lead pencil which dangled from his watch-chain.

"It is an interesting record," he muttered, running his eye over the page, "and when the credit entries are made, it will be more interesting still. My time will come—I feel it! I am free-born,—I am rich—I am as white as they; and I have been better educated. Yet they treat me like a Negro, and when I am struck I cannot return the blow, under pain of losing my liberty or my life. Ah, could I but face them as man to man!" he cried, putting his hand to his side, upon an imaginary sword-hilt. "But I forget—*nom de Dieu*—a man of color cannot bear arms! But we shall see! We shall see!"

"What insolence!" cried old Zabet, insinuatingly, as the other gentleman, maintaining his position upon the sidewalk, still stared across toward the cathedral door into which the Spaniard and his daughter were disappearing.

The gentleman, absorbed in his own thoughts, made no reply.

"What heavenly beauty, Monsieur Raoul!" crooned the old woman.

The young man glanced at the speaker. The white girl had gone in, and the old brown woman offered a ready foil to her radiant youth and beauty. Nevertheless his irritation had not yet subsided, and he only scowled at the old cake-woman.

"If only justice were done, Monsieur Raoul," Zabet, intent upon her own purpose, persisted, "and you, as the eldest born, were acknowledged as your uncle's heir, you would not need to look at her from a distance. I saw old Miché Pierre this morning. He is in a bad way, poor man!"

"How so, Zabet?" demanded the gentleman, his brow clearing somewhat at the old woman's words. "Is it his heart, or his gout, or both together?"

Zabet shook her head with a portentous sigh.

"His gout, Monsieur Raoul, is threatening his heart. And his spirits are low. He complains that his nephews do not love him, that they neglect their old uncle, that they seldom come near him."

Raoul Beaurepas, sugar and cotton broker, roué and speculator, who had just received a call for additional margins to save him from a loss which threatened bankruptcy, jumped at the hook, like a hungry fish at a fat worm. Another silver piece found lodgment in Zabet's basket. The younger Beaurepas were prodigal, while their money lasted.

"*Merci*, Zabet, he shall no longer complain. When is he in the most amiable mood?"

"In the afternoon, Monsieur Raoul, after his siesta, you will make a better impression."

II.

THE PROPHECY

Flushed with prosperity, Zabet began to give away cakes to several little half-naked pot-bellied black children who were eyeing her basket wistfully. This altruistic pastime was interrupted by the return of the young man who had received the blow from Raoul Beaurepas.

With downcast eyes, and looking neither to right nor left, he was passing old Zabet without looking at her, when he heard himself called, in insinuating tones:

"Oh, Miché!—Monsieur Marchand!—oh, master!"

The young man thus accosted, who was known as Paul Marchand, hesitated. The old woman had witnessed his humiliation, but her form of address was music to the quadroon ear. He turned and approached her.

"What is it, Tante Zabet?"

"I dreamed about you last night, Miché."

"You dream too much, Tante Zabet,—about things which do not concern you."

"But, Miché, it was a beautiful dream. If it came true, it would make you very happy."

"Who said I am not happy?"

"Ah, Miché, how can you be happy? Did I not see just now? Do I not know?"

"I have wealth."

"Small wealth, Miché! Old Pierre Beaurepas has ten times as much."

"It is enough, and more than most. I have a beautiful wife who loves me dearly, and whom I love no less."

"She is a quadroon, monsieur, and you are white, at least to look at—you could pass for white. You have no mark of color—you could have been a gentleman, monsieur! There are others no whiter!"

Marchand sighed. He had married for love, and his wife had brought him wealth from her white father—a dozen houses, a ship, a warehouse stocked with merchandise, and money in the funds. Marchand loved Julie very deeply. What old Zabet had said was true—he might have passed for white, had he so chosen in time. His paternity he did not know. His mother he had never seen; she had died, he understood, in his infancy. He had been brought up by an elderly quadroon woman, one Angeline Dufour, and his support had been provided by a lawyer of the city, a certain M. Jules Renard, a well known Creole advocate, with a large practice in the French quarter. M. Renard had never acknowledged the paternity of young Marchand, nor indeed had it ever been attributed to him. When questioned once by the lad upon the subject, he had answered, somewhat curtly, that Marchand should take the gifts the gods provided, and be thankful and not curious; that his support came from a fund, left to him, M. Renard, as trustee, by a philanthropic gentleman who had known his mother many years before. With this Marchand was forced to be content. That he had not been born in wedlock, as he naturally assumed, gave him little concern; no quadroon was, except in marriage between members of his own class, and he was not the fruit of such a union, and what was shared by all was not a source of shame or disgrace, which are always grounded in some departure from the normal. And in that day there were great men of irregular birth. Many escutcheons of the aristocracy of Europe were crossed by the bar sinister. The Latin mind has ever been tender toward the sins of love and youth and hot blood, and correspondingly merciful toward their fruit. The strain of African blood was infinitely more damning—it could never, in Louisiana, be lived down, unless its possessor should, where possible, leave the neighborhood where he was reared, and, to use an expression still in vogue in our own day, pass for white.

The trust fund administered by M. Renard had fed and clothed young Marchand, had sent him, when he approached manhood, to school in Paris, where he had spent several happy years, finding, in the free atmosphere of student life in the French capital, the opportunity to expand in mind and spirit. There was no color line in France, nor ever has been, and in that country men of color even at that epoch had occasionally distinguished themselves in war, in art, in letters and in politics. His schooling completed, he had remained in Paris until, at the suggestion of M. Renard, he had returned to New Orleans.

Among the passengers on the voyage homeward was Julie Lenoir, the quadroon daughter of Jacques Lenoir, a wealthy New Orleans Creole, by a beloved mistress. Old Lenoir had never married, and upon his death, which had occurred while Julie was still a pupil at the convent in Paris, where she had been sent for her education, had left his entire fortune to his daughter Julie and her younger sister Lizette.

In Paris Julie and Paul had met no difference in treatment because of their color, but when they set foot on an American ship, their origin being known, they were left almost entirely to themselves by the other passengers and therefore instinctively fell back upon each other for companionship during the long voyage. It was before the advent of the steamboat and a sailing vessel consumed from three to six weeks in crossing the Atlantic. Youth, propinquity, sympathy, had their innings, with the result that the two young people fell in love and were married shortly after the vessel arrived at New Orleans.

The care of his wife's property, which under his capable management was rapidly increasing in value, had furnished Marchand with wholesome occupation, and he could have remained in New Orleans indefinitely, to his financial profit, had it not been for the conditions under which he, like others of his kind, were obliged to live, of which his treatment by Hector Beaurepas on the street in front of the cathedral was an illustration, although an aggravated one, and for which his sojourn in France had entirely unfitted him. No white man had ever struck him before; perhaps none would ever strike him again; but that it could be done, and he could not resent it, were gall and wormwood to him.

Endowed with an energy and an initiative which, had he been entirely white, would have rendered him notable among the easy-going Creoles, he had found it difficult to keep strictly within the lines prescribed for those of his caste, and had at times presumed upon his fairness of complexion to exercise, in company where he was not known, privileges reserved by law or by custom for white men only. Under the old Spanish and French regimes, this might have been done with comparative ease, but, with the American annexation and the ensuing influx of Americans from other states, there had come a hardening of racial lines, and a growing intolerance toward the free colored population. A group of young men, American and Creole, among whom several of the Beaurepas cousins were prominent, had constituted themselves champions of the white race and were always on the alert to rebuke presumption on the part of any mulatto or quadroon. Thus it was almost inevitable that Paul Merchand, by his foreign education and his wife's wealth the most conspicuous young man of his class in the city, and with the proud and sensitive spirit he had inherited from some unknown ancestor, should at some time or other come in contact with one or the other of the Beaurepas, and, with the tremendous odds against him, equally certain that he should have the worst of any such encounter.

"You are no prophet, Zabet," said Marchand, "if you can only tell me what might have been. You can tell me nothing that I do not know already. I have wealth, health, youth, a good education, a loving wife, and I have two bright and beautiful children, than whom there are none lovelier."

"Whom you cannot send to the Ursuline Convent, who cannot sit in a box at the Opera. Your children should be sought after, monsieur, by the best in the land. They will be, no doubt, but not as you would wish."

"*Tais-toi!* Be silent! old croaker! I have had enough to bear for one day, and I have affairs to attend to."

"Tarry a moment, monsieur,—master,—and I will tell your fortune, as I saw it in a dream—only last night—I swear it! It was an auspicious fortune. Be patient for a moment; I am growing old, and my memory is not what it was." She paused significantly.

"Hurry, old woman, with your nonsense! This will refresh your memory." He tossed a piece of silver into Zabet's basket.

"*Bien merci, Miché!* God prosper you! It will buy liniment for my rheumatism. This is your fortune: You are rich, you shall be richer. You are proud, you shall be prouder. You are white, you shall be whiter. You have a handsome wife, you shall have one more beautiful. You have lovely children; you shall have others more lovely. And—you have been insulted, you shall be avenged!"

The quadroon smiled sadly.

"Your dream is only a dream, Zabet!" he said, "and for the most part not a pleasant dream. I hope to be richer, of course, if my affairs are successful—that goes without saying. I can be no whiter, for I could not be born again, and if I could, a man may not choose his color. There is no place for pride, and little for self-respect, in a quadroon's life. Your dream would make me lose my wife, and there is no better wife in New Orleans. But you have promised me revenge, Zabet, and for that I should like to believe at least that much, of your prophecy, for I myself have dreamed of it."

"It will all come true, Miché. There are dreams and dreams, and this is a true one—a prophecy, a revelation—you may trust old Zabet. *Adieu, Miché! Merci, Miché!*"

The young man had tossed another coin into her basket as he moved away.

The brief service in the cathedral was over by this time, and the congregation dispersing. Among the first to come out, having been of the last to enter and therefore among those seated nearest the door, were the old Spaniard and his beautiful daughter. The gentleman helped the girl into the carriage; and following her, took the reins from the colored lad who had been holding them, to whom he gave a small copper coin, which was immediately spent with Zabet for sweet cakes. The Spaniard's horse, a superannuated thoroughbred, started forward at a leisurely pace.

A singularly graceful young man, of the Creole type, at the same moment entered the Square at the side opposite that from which the Spaniard's carriage was leaving. At sight of the vehicle, he quickened his pace to a run and followed it.

"Miché Philippe! Miché Philippe!" called old Zabet after him. But he was gone.

The old cake woman threw a softened look after him.

"There he goes," she muttered, "after old Jose Morales and his beautiful daughter. He does not like me, Miché Philippe, but I pray for him every night, and I have promised ten candles to Ste. Anne if she will keep him from harm, and make Miché Pierre leave him a fortune."

Upon leaving old Zabet, Paul Marchand turned the next corner, and, pursued his way along the Rue Toulouse, until he came to a small brick house, with its end to the street, a balcony overhead, and a door at the side leading through a brick wall into a garden from which admittance was gained to the house. It was the residence and *atélier* of Guillaume Perigord, the most popular *maître-d'armes* or fencing master of the day, under whose tuition the gilded youth of New Orleans studied the use of the rapier and the etiquette of the duello, a relic of the feudal system which still remained a popular pastime and was destined to linger yet a while.

The young man knocked at the gate, which was opened by a black servant. A broad-shouldered, athletic Frenchman, somewhat under the medium height, with fierce mustachios and bristling black hair sprinkled with gray, came forward with every evidence of cordiality.

"*Bon jour,* M. Marchand! *Comment ça va?* I hope you carry yourself well today," he exclaimed warmly.

"Miserably, Perigord, miserably. I have just been insulted by a blackguard,—a *soi-disant* gentleman."

"And you wish me to act as your second? You will run him through?"

"No, Perigord, this is not Paris. There I was a free man, a gentleman. Here I am a quadroon—a man of color—without rights that a white man is bound to respect."

"*Pardieu,* Monsieur, I believe it is so, but, it is a shame! A great shame! *Sacre nom d'un chien!* You should go back to Paris, Monsieur, where a man is a man. I learned the *art d'escrime* from the mulatto Chevalier St. Georges, the finest fencing master of Paris, the friend of the Regent and of Madame. I fought in Egypt under General Dumas, the hero of the Tyrol, the mulatto friend of Napoleon. They were better men than these who flout you, Monsieur."

"Thank you, Perigord. They lived in France, where they could be men. When can you come to my house?"

"Whenever you say, except during my business hours. But why cannot monsieur have his practice here? I can teach you nothing but a trick or two. My Paris predecessor has made you already the best swordsman in New Orleans."

"You flatter me, Perigord. I cannot stand up against you, and I wish to keep up and to improve my skill. You had better come to my house. It would do you no good to have it known that you taught a quadroon an art which he is forbidden by law to exercise. At five o'clock, at my house, by the garden gate. *Au revoir,* Perigord."

Marchand went away.

"He is a great fool," remarked Perigord, lighting a long black cigar. "He is a great fool to stay here, when he has money and could live in France. But Louisiana is full of fools. The grandsons of adventurers and *filles à la cassette* who people Louisiana, look down upon me, the grandson of a Marquis, and a veteran of the Grand Army. A wise man would be lonesome in Louisiana."

A few days after the events in the *vieux carré* above recorded, the quadroon Marchand had an altercation, at the cotton exchange, which might have had consequences which would have put an end to all of his problems by putting an end to Marchand himself.

It was the outgrowth, in effect, of old Zabet's dream, which seemed, for a while, by way of bringing in its train the greatest of ill fortune,—for the reason, no doubt, that dreams go by contraries. Rolling under his tongue like a sweet morsel the old woman's prophecy—which he enjoyed without at all believing it,—he had for the time being almost forgotten that he was a quadroon, and that the path which he must walk, in his intercourse with white men, was a straight and narrow one, from which he must deviate neither to the right nor to the left. He was bidding one day for some cotton on the exchange, with which to complete a consignment to his factor in Liverpool. It had been knocked down to his bid, when Hector Beaurepas, who had been bidding against him, claimed the bid as his own. Marchand protested with more heat than prudence.

"I beg your pardon, *Monsieur,*" he said, "the bid was mine."

"It was mine," declared Beaurepas rudely. "The auctioneer knows it was mine."

The auctioneer hesitated. He knew it was Marchand's bid, but the controversy was that of quadroon with white man. Marchand saw him wavering.

"It was mine," he insisted. "The gentleman knows it was mine."

Beaurepas made a movement as if to draw the blade from the sword-cane which he carried, but did not complete it.

"*Cochon!*" he cried, "pig of a Negro! Would you call me a liar? The bid was mine and the auctioneer will so declare it. I should like to slit your ears, if it would not soil my sword. It might improve your hearing."

"It is an outrage," murmured one man to another. "It was Marchand's bid."

"It was not the conduct of a gentleman," responded the man addressed. "*Noblesse oblige,* when the other is without redress."

But their remarks, which might have served somewhat as balm to Marchand's wounded spirit, were not spoken in his hearing, and meantime, filled with mortification and with futile rage, he had turned away, with a very poor attempt at dignity. For how could any man, unless he were a hero, or a martyr to a cause—and Marchand was neither,—how could any one move with dignity among those in whose presence one had just been called a pig and had another threaten to slit his ears, nay, even announce that his touch would be pollution, if but for the purpose of performing upon him a surgical operation which even a gentleman might presumably perform upon a pig, without defilement;—when the conditions were such that he might not resent the insult?

Poor Marchand! It was a hard world, and only some strain in his nature, odd for one of his upbringing, saved him from self-pity, the most unmanly of sentiments. Consumed with rage, he could only suffer in silence. He could not find relief by speaking to any white Creole, for however much some of them might have sympathized with him, they could not have taken his part without a breach of caste. Marchand would not take his grievance to his colored friends; he would not care to have them know that he had been so humiliated. Instinctively he held himself a little above all but a few of them. Moreover, they would not have understood the intensity of his feeling. They were even more easy-going than their white neighbors, adding to the Creole lack of energy the even greater languor of the African. They were philosophical enough to recognize the existence of facts as they were, and conform to them as the price of life and some degree of comfort. Indeed some of them already regarded Marchand as a not altogether safe representative of their class, who was likely, by his truculence, to stir up feeling against the rest of them. So Marchand could only rage to his wife, Julie, and find in her sweet sympathy such solace as he might, and make another entry on his tablets, large letters, heavily underscored.

III.

M. Pierre Beaurepas

When Adolphe Beaurepas, following the suggestion made by Zabet Philosophe the day before, ascended the steps of his uncle's mansion the next morning about ten o'clock, his bosom was fluttering with hope. His uncle's house, the temple of the Beaurepas cult, stood on Royal Street, a block from the Place d'Armes and a little to the south of the Cathedral. It had been built by Antoine Beaurepas, the father of Pierre, of limestone brought from France in his own bottoms, with a tiled roof, a vaulted entrance leading to a large paved court surrounded by broad galleries or verandahs with wrought-iron railings,—perhaps the finest example in the city of the older style of architecture, destined, in the newer American section across Canal Street, to give way ere long to the so called Colonial style, with its Ionic or Corinthian columns, which afterwards became so common in the Southern states.

A dignified, elderly mulatto admitted Adolphe, who spoke kindly to the servant, his uncle's butler, factotum and favorite—a good friend to have at court.

"Good morning, Terence. I hope you are well?"

"Passably well, Miché Adolphe."

"And my excellent uncle—I am sure you take good care of him?"

"He does not complain of me, sir."

"I should like to pay him my respects, Terence. By the way, I know you like a good cigar. These are pure Cubanos, worth their weight in silver."

The butler bowed, and bestowed the cigar carefully in his vest pocket.

"*Merci,* Miché Adolphe. I will announce you."

Adolphe, left alone in the hall, threw around him a look of hungry interest. The polished floor was dotted with costly Persian rugs. The walls of the spacious apartment were hung in part with fine reproductions, in the Aubusson weave, of the set of Gobelin tapestries illustrating episodes in the life of Alexander the Great. The ceiling was a fresco, after Boucher, of the Judgment of Paris. On one side a famous Velasquez looked down at him, there was a painting of Vigée Lebrun, and, among other family portraits, one of old Pierre himself, painted by David during one of the rich colonial's frequent visits to Paris in former years. The furniture was Louis Quinze. There was a large Boulle cabinet, in ebony, on which stood a silver casket, the handiwork of Benvenuto Cellini, flanked by several rare seventeenth century bronzes. It was the abode of wealth informed by culture and refined by taste, though there was a noticeable absence of the feminine touch, for old Pierre Beaurepas was a widower of long standing. He had married for love, in middle life, under somewhat romantic circumstances, and when, after some years, his wife, whose slightest whim had been law to one of the hardest men in New Orleans in his dealings with other men, died and left him childless, he remained faithful to her memory and never sought to fill her place. Old Terence, though a slave a man of capacity and fair education, with a staff of male and female subordinates conducted the establishment in accordance with the habits and wishes of his master.

Adolphe, waiting, appraised the paintings, the tapestries and the furniture, with which he was very familiar, having been brought up among them, and imagined himself the owner. He could live very comfortably in the midst of them, or find a use for the money they would bring, should he be lucky enough to be his uncle's heir.

Terence returned ere long.

"The master will see you, sir. Follow me."

The library, into which the servant led the way, was a large room behind the salon, looking out upon the paved courtyard. The walls were lined with glazed bookcases, filled with leather-backed books, many of them bound in hand-tooled morocco. There were some choice etchings and wood engravings, and, on a mahogany pedestal a reduced copy, in bronze, of Houdon's seated statue of Voltaire. Adolphe knew the books by their titles, but had small familiarity with their contents; he had never been fond of reading. Many of them he was aware were rare and curious, and should they become his, they could readily be turned into money which would buy pleasures he would appreciate far more than those of the intellect.

The old gentleman into whose presence Adolphe Beaurepas was ushered, and whom he saluted with every outward sign of affection and reverence, was seated in an arm-chair beside an open window. Old and ailing as he was, in the well-cut nose, the high and slightly receding forehead, crowned by a profusion of white hair which fell to his shoulders, the strong chin, which was clean shaven, the thin lips and high cheekbones, the grey eyes, of which age had but slightly dimmed the luster, Adolphe could see the wreck of the virile, capable man of affairs, the disciple of Rousseau and Voltaire, cynical in his attitude toward life, none too trustful of his fellow men, that Pierre Beaurepas had been in his prime. He displayed in his old age, to those with whom he came in contact, that air of assured position, or perhaps assured possessions, which comes to those who have been successful and retain the fruits of success. At his elbow stood a small table, upon which were a flask of Chambertin, a meerschaum pipe, a bowl of tobacco, and a manual of chess, in French. In his hand he held a copy of *Émile*, autographed and annotated by the great Jean Jacques himself, which Beaurepas had received from his Parisian bookseller only the day before—a rare item for his collection.

Old Pierre Beaurepas was the wealthiest Creole in New Orleans. His ancestor, Count Armand de Beaurepas, had helped Bienville to lay the foundations of the colony, and had profited by valuable land grants and trading monopolies. A later Beaurepas had been in Paris at the height of John Law's colossal speculation. A prudent man, and better informed than most Europeans of the real resources of the colony, he held his tongue, bought shares in the Mississippi Company, sold before the bubble burst, and realized five hundred per cent on his investment. Several citizens of Paris, who claimed that they had been advised by him to invest in Law's scheme, expressed themselves, after the disaster, with considerable ferocity concerning the colonial Beaurepas and what they would like to do to him; but since the gentleman, with commendable prudence, had already returned to his home beyond the seas, their objurgations fell upon the empty air. At the time of our story the Beaurepas estate, by successive accretions, due to conservative management, natural growth and wise and fortunate investments had attained large proportions. By a family custom, based on feudal tradition, following the law of primogeniture, the bulk of the estate had always passed to the eldest son or male representative. But since the American occupation and its attendant changes, the old Creole customs had shown a tendency to relax, and whether the traditional succession of the Beaurepas estate would be at all altered upon the death of old Pierre, was a question of great importance to several citizens of New Orleans, for more than one reason, the chief of these being that old Pierre Beaurepas was childless, and possessed, therefore, no direct heir.

The succession lay among his five nephews. Pierre had married, at forty, the childless widow of Maxime Ledoux, a friend of his youth, and at one time his partner in business. The lady's second marriage proved no more fruitful than her first. Pierre Beaurepas had had two younger brothers, Reneé and Louis, who owned estates in Hayti, the fairest and richest of the French colonies. Prior to the revolution in that unhappy island they had lived in luxury upon their revenues. The two brothers and their wives had been massacred, with most of the other whites of the island. Their children, two of one brother and three of the other, had escaped only through the devotion of their colored nurse, Zabet, who had also tried to save the parents, but in vain. She had fled with other refugees, and after incredible hardships had reached New Orleans, where she had turned over to Pierre Beaurepas the children, as the sole survivors of the Haytian branch of the family, and herself, as the sole remnant of the Haytian estates. Since that time, while she had never received any formal deed of manumission, on the other hand no steps had been taken to administer her as part of the estate of the deceased Haytian Beaurepas, and she had remained, in recognition of her services, to all intents and purposes a free woman—at any rate a masterless slave—a sort of human *chose in action*, which had never been reduced to possession. She could not have proved her freedom; nor, on the other hand, had any one ever claimed her as a slave.

Old Pierre Beaurepas had acquitted himself generously toward his orphan nephews. They were brought up in the house on Royal Street. They were sent to good schools, and each one, upon reaching his majority, was given sufficient money to set himself up in the business of his choice, well fortified in addition by their uncle's example and his oft-repeated precepts. No one of them had ever been named or suggested as the heir. Perhaps this very fact was in large measure responsible for the further fact that not one of them had made a brilliant success in business. Had old Pierre specifically designated any one of his nephews as his successor, the remaining four would in all likelihood have applied their fair native abilities to business, with the hope of finding through this channel the way to wealth and honors. But how could one reasonably expect a Creole, of Gallic blood and imagination, softened by the languors of a sub-tropical climate, to struggle painfully toward the heights of life, while there was one chance in five that he might ride thither in a golden chariot, behind a black driver in livery?

Old Pierre had fostered no such illusion on the part of his nephews. On the contrary, he had distinctly informed each of them, upon establishing him in business, that he must make his own way and that the money thus given must not be regarded as an advance upon any future inheritance. But Pierre Beaurepas was eccentric, and supposed not always to mean everything that he said. Moreover, such a statement could not be accepted as conclusive. It was clear that some one must inherit the estate. It was equally obvious that the estate must descend to a Beaurepas, and that there were no possible heirs except the five nephews of the present owner. There was enough to have made them all rich, though it was not conceivable that the estate would be divided.

Without spending a great deal of time, however, in discussing the psychology of the situation, it is nevertheless true that upon this pleasant day when Adolphe Beaurepas entered his uncle's house, the plantation of which he was the nominal owner was mortgaged to the limit of its security value, with foreclosure imminent; that Raoul Beaurepas had used the funds of his firm for his own purposes and was threatened with exposure, unless a miracle should happen; that the business house of which Hector Beaurepas was the head was on the verge of bankruptcy; that Henri Beaurepas owed more debts than he could ever hope to pay out of his income; and when it is borne in mind that old Pierre Beaurepas was in feeble health, his heart action weak, and his gout severe; and when it is further considered that no one of his nephews dared to approach him for aid, for fear that such a step might jeopardize his heirship, it is clearly apparent that there was occasion for considerable anxiety in the minds of the younger Beaurepas. The uncertainty of the situation was sufficient, however, to give them a desperate hold upon solvency—each one was able to inspire his creditors with some of his own hopefulness, and to pacify them pending the outcome of their uncle's illness.

The rainbow of hope had appeared faintly upon Adolphe Beaurepas's financial horizon during his interview with Zabet Philosophe in the morning. During the few hours which had elapsed before his visit to his uncle's house, the arc of promise had grown more and more distinct; and when, upon being ushered into his uncle's presence, old Pierre greeted his nephew with outstretched hand and a contortion of the facial muscles which might have been analyzed, by those who knew the grim old Creole, as something akin to a smile, Adolphe felt a sudden elation inspiring in its quality. The rainbow had led him to the pot of gold.

Old Pierre had not risen from his armchair. His swollen foot, thickly swathed in bandages, rested upon a cushioned footstool. After a first shrewd glance at his nephew, who had greeted him with ceremonious deference, he then, without further preliminaries, demanded of Adolphe how his business was progressing, and whether he could be of any service to him.

Adolphe took heart of courage. That his uncle should manifest this special interest in him was extremely significant. That his uncle should already have informed himself concerning his affairs was quite likely. But if his uncle were ignorant, would it be wise to deceive him, thereby hoping to win a reputation for business acumen which might commend him to his uncle? His uncle might wish to leave the Beaurepas estate in the hands of a successful business man, by whom he might feel sure it would be wisely administered. But on the other hand, should his uncle discover the deceit which had been practiced upon him, which he could easily do if he wished, the consequences might prove disastrous. No, his uncle Pierre evidently felt a personal interest, a hitherto dormant affection waking into activity toward his favorite nephew, Adolphe. This was a time for frank confession; not too frank, of course—his uncle did not need to know that his embarrassment had been brought about by a reckless speculation; he might be left to infer that it was the result of conditions beyond his nephew's control.

Adolphe told his story. His affairs were prosperous; his prospects were more than fair; but there had been unforeseen complications, which he referred to somewhat vaguely—to his relief his uncle did not press him for details; a temporary loan which he hoped to negotiate somewhere, would tide him over his difficulties.

Old Pierre listened with imperturbable gravity. Adolphe, charmed by his uncle's receptiveness, and engrossed in the construction of a work of fiction, did not observe the old man's eye reading him through and through. It would have taken a more accomplished liar than Adolphe Beaurepas to deceive this seasoned veteran of the market-place.

"And how much, my dear Adolphe," he demanded softly, "would be required to relieve you from this temporary embarrassment?"

Adolphe's inward glow at this inquiry was reflected in his beaming countenance. He had come expecting at least a lecture, instead of which he was offered a loan. He indulged in a moment of rapid reflection. His uncle had practically handed him a blank check. He needed about ten thousand dollars. If he asked for twenty thousand it might be too much. In the middle path there was safety.

"About fifteen thousand dollars, my dear uncle, carefully employed, would carry me well over my present difficulties."

"Ah, well, Adolphe," returned the old gentleman, "to one of my age the sole remaining source of happiness is to make others happy. Some day, perhaps not many years hence, I must die, and my estate must have an heir. I do not wish the name of Beaurepas to be discredited. The man who would inherit my estate must keep his financial honor unsullied."

He rang the silver bell which stood upon the table by his side. His mulatto servant appeared.

"Terence, my check book."

The servant brought the book, and old Pierre drew a check on the Bank of New Orleans for fifteen thousand dollars, to the order of Adolphe Beaurepas.

"You might give me," said the uncle, "a written acknowledgment. It is, of course, between us a mere formality. But an old man cannot change the business habits of a lifetime. An ordinary promissory note will be sufficient."

"Within what time shall I make it payable?

"A year?" suggested his uncle.

Adolphe reflected. His uncle could not last three months, six months would leave a wide margin of safety. The more transitory his difficulties were made to seem, the better impression would remain.

"We can easily repay the loan within six months," he said, "I will make the note for that period."

He thanked his uncle profusely, and took his departure, fully convinced that he would be the Beaurepas heir, and that the fifteen thousand dollars was merely a pitiful advance upon a great inheritance.

As Adolphe passed through the gate, into the street, he met Zabet Philosophe entering with her basket upon her head.

"*Bon jour,* Miché Adolphe," she said, dropping him a curtsey.

"*Bon jour,* Zabet," said Adolphe, beaming upon the old woman. "Your dream has come true. You are a wise old witch. Here is a dollar for you."

He tossed the coin toward the old woman and went his way, absorbed in dreams of wealth and grandeur. The money fell upon the ground. Zabet stopped somewhat stiffly, picked it up with some difficulty, and dropped it in her capacious pocket. It would buy her another lottery ticket and give her another chance at the capital prize. Then, depositing her basket in the yard, she entered the house and was shown into the old man's presence.

"Adolphe has just left me," he said.

"Yes, master, I met him at the door."

"Have you seen them all, Zabet?" he demanded.

"Yes, master, the rest will all be here. I have seen to it that they shall."

"Do you ever see the young man, Marchand, Zabet?"

"Yes, master."

"Is he well?"

"Perfectly well, Master Pierre."

"And successful in his affairs?"

"Quite so. He seems to have rare good fortune."

"Is he happy?"

The old woman shrugged her shoulders.

"How could he be happy, Master Pierre, in New Orleans?"

She related to the old man the scene on the *vieux carré* in which Marchand and Raoul Beaurepas had taken part.

The old man frowned.

"Raoul has a bad temper," he observed. "I fear he is not quite a gentleman. I suspect he associates too freely with the *sacrés Americains* who infest our city. No Creole of the older generation would have done such a thing. But advise the young man, when you find occasion, to be patient and to do nothing rash. His case may seem a hopeless one, but miracles have been known to happen. And let me know at once if he should get into any serious difficulty."

"*Très bien*, Miché Pierre, I shall watch him closely."

Before the close of the day the four Beaurepas cousins to whom Zabet had spoken on the *vieux carrée* had called upon their uncle. What happened with Adolphe we have already seen. To each of the others Old Pierre gave as seemingly cordial a reception. Each was encouraged to disclose the state of his affairs. To each according to his apparent need, the uncle had offered aid, and from each had taken a note of hand for the amount loaned—a proceeding at which each nephew smiled to himself, reflecting that the force of habit was strong with uncle Pierre, and that while the old man's purpose was obvious, his characteristic secretiveness would not permit him to state it clearly. This conclusion on the part of each nephew that *he* was the favorite nephew and prospective heir, was emphasized and made certain by the request which old Pierre made of each that he should say nothing to any of the others concerning the matter in which he had been favored.

Each of the nephews had been advised by their uncle to use this money carefully. Each observed the avuncular injunction according to his personal idiosyncracy. Adolphe Beaurepas paid off the mortgage on his plantation, which amounted to ten thousand dollars, but, instead of holding the remaining five thousand in reserve against future contingencies, embarked in another speculation, which proved a failure and left him merely square with the world, except for the debt to his uncle, which caused him no uneasiness. He was not a married man—none of the nephews were married. That their uncle meant his heir to marry Josephine Morales was known to them all, a plan which could not be carried out unless the heir were an unmarried man. Naturally of a secretive, mole-like disposition, it was no trouble for Adolphe to observe his uncle's wish and keep his own counsel, which he did, and dreamed of future opulence.

Hector Beaurepas paid off the more pressing of his debts, and immediately began to contract large additional obligations. Raoul made good his speculations. Henri bought his mistress a new wardrobe, and spent the rest at roulette in a certain gambling den on Canal Street, backing a system which he had figured out to a mathematical certainty would break the bank. But, apart from any resultant evidences of prosperity, there was a general increase among the nephews of pride and self-importance, which, had it been confined to any single one of them, would have been quite noticeable to the others. That they did not observe it was due to the fact that each of them had shifted his own position to the same viewpoint. It was, of course, perfectly natural that their scale of living and expenditure should increase. The prospective heir of the wealthiest man in New Orleans must live on a scale commensurate with his expectations. Each Beaurepas, therefore, wondered at the extravagance of the others, and deplored with complacent sadness the ultimate certainty of their disappointment; nor, because of the promise made to their uncle, could he warn them against the consequences of a prodigality which their uncle's intention would not justify.

Meantime, old Pierre Beaurepas clung tenaciously though feebly to life. He had lived through three-quarters of the hundred years that made up the life of the city. He had seen it bandied from nation to nation,—from France to Spain, from Spain to France, from France to the United States. He had seen it grow from a small provincial settlement in a fever-ridden marsh until it was obviously destined to become one of the greatest cities of the continent. For more than forty years he had been a power in the commercial and social life of the city, and he wished to carry on as long as he might. To live might demand a struggle, but—*le jeu valait la chandelle*—the prize was worth the effort. He maintained a healthy interest in business and went down once or twice a month to his office in the Bank of New Orleans, of which he was the largest stockholder and a director. Meantime his heir might wait—the inheritance was well worth

house with the slave quarters grouped around or near it, and dark-hued laborers toiling with plow or hoe. Philippe was astride of a good horse, the road was dry, the morning fair, there was an aromatic breeze from over the river and all nature was in tune with his mood, and as he rode he sang:

> " 'Delaide, mo la reine,
> Chimin-la trop longue pour alle:-
> Chimin-la monte dans les hauts;
> Tout piti qui mo ye,
> M'alle monte la haut dans courant,
>   C'est moin, Liron, qui rive
>   M'alle di ye,
>   Bonsoir, mo la reine,
>   C'est moin, Liron, qui rive."

> " 'Delaide, my queen, the way is long,
> That leads upstream to thee,
> But, though I'm small, the current strong
> Will be as naught to me.
>   " 'Tis I, Liron, who come,
>   I come to thee,
>   Good night, my queen!
>   'Tis I, Liron, who come."

At Trois Pigeons dwelt Don José Morales, in the large, sprawling, substantially built in the Spanish fashion but now somewhat dilapidated frame house erected by his father fifty years before. It was neither the house, however, nor old Don José that drew Philippe Beaurepas toward Trois Pigeons. The magnet which attracted him was none other than Joséphine, Don José's seventeen-year old daughter, born when he was past fifty, cherished by him as the apple of his eye and also as his chief bulwark against ever-encroaching bankruptcy.

Don José Morales was the bosom friend of old Pierre

Beaurepas. It was not, upon the surface, a well-assorted friendship. Pierre Beaurepas, as we have seen, was the wealthiest man in New Orleans. Don José, in spite of his ancient name and Spanish pride, was known to be in perennial hard luck. The plantation had been mortgaged for two generations. From whatever defect of skill or ability, Don José usually failed where others succeeded. If his next door neighbor made a good crop of indigo, the Morales growth would either prove a failure in the field or be spoiled in the manufacture. When other planters changed to cane and began to boil sugar, Don José clung to indigo. If he speculated in cotton he was always caught on the losing side of the market. His slaves bred poorly and were subject to epidemics that carried them off like sick cattle. They even took the yellow fever, to which most blacks were immune. One year the sugar-house had been burned; another year a crevasse in the levee had inundated the plantation.

Pierre Beaurepas held the mortgage on Trois Pigeons, in spite of which the friendship remained unbroken, a most remarkable circumstance when the deadly effect of debt upon friendship is borne in mind. Who avoids one so much as he who owes him five dollars or ten? If so small a sum can have so potent an influence, what must be said of a friendship which can survive the consciousness, upon the one hand, that one's debtor is embarrassed and one's security doubtful, and upon the other that one is at the mercy of his creditor?

The most essential element of friendship is equality. That this particular friendship should survive under these conditions, was due to the fact that it was rooted in matters more vital than those which dealt with gold. Even the most sentimental of Creoles would have smiled at the suggestion that to José Morales, always in debt, or to Pierre Beaurepas, landlord and moneylender, anything could be more important than gold. And yet there was a romance in their lives. Years before, when both were young, they had been comrades in an expedition against the pirates who from time to time, during a period of years, infested the lower Mississippi. In an encounter with these miscreants, José Morales had interposed his own body to receive the stroke of a cutlass aimed at the head of Pierre Beaurepas, who lay stunned and senseless upon the deck of the good ship *Bon Espoir*. Pierre Beaurepas had always remembered the obligation and had never considered the debt as paid. It was the one sentimental episode, except his marriage, so far as any one knew, that had marked the career of this keenest of New Orleans business men. If there had been another, as may appear, it had not been for the public.

For many years the two men, living in the same city neighborhood, had seen one another almost daily. When Don José had given up his town house and gone to live entirely on his plantation, and Pierre's health had begun to fail, they still exchanged visits at least once a month. They were both expert chess-players, and if the game were not completed at the end of a meeting, the positions would be noted and the contest resumed when next they came together. If Morales were ever unable to pay the interest on the mortgage, his friend merely charged it against him on the ledger. Neither of them seemed to worry about the future.

"My heir," said Pierre, "shall marry your daughter. The mortgage will thus merge into the estate."

"She shall marry no other man, I swear," Morales was wont to answer.

When Joséphine was twelve years old she gave promise of unusual beauty.

"My heir will be a very fortunate man," said old Pierre

one day to his friend, glancing at the maid with rare appreciation.

"Which of your nephews is to be the heir?" Morales asked, removing his long black cigar from his lips. "The girl is approaching womanhood, and it would be well to guide her fancy in the right direction. You have several handsome nephews."

"Tell her, José, to keep her heart free! But she is still a child, and perhaps it would be better to tell her nothing. I have not yet named my heir."

Joséphine was a pupil of the Ursuline Convent. Had she been kept always under lock and key, perhaps her heart might have remained entirely free. But her mother was dead, and her father not inordinately strict. She had many opportunities to meet young people, especially the Beaurepas cousins. They had played together as children, before Señor Morales had sold his town house and taken up his residence at Trois Pigeons. She had always thought Philippe the handsomest of the lot, and Philippe, while yet a lad, had perceived, with the temperamental precociousness of the sub-tropics, that Joséphine was beautiful. More than once he had told her so.

"Joséphine," he would say, "you are the most beautiful of women. I love you and wish more than anything else in the world to marry you."

"Hush, Philippe," she had replied, "you must not say such things to me. My father has promised your uncle that I shall marry his heir."

"And why may I not be the heir?" demanded Philippe, stoutly. Until Joséphine raised it, the question of the inheritance had never been considered very seriously by Philippe. It was a pleasing possibility but he had not built upon it. He had been bred a gentlemen, had been educated, clothed and nurtured as a gentleman, and expected by his own exertions to be able to live as a gentleman. He had no expensive vices—he was neither drunkard, nor gambler, nor roué. But after Joséphine had spoken thus, the inheritance assumed an added value in his eyes. To be his uncle's heir was to marry Joséphine; not to be the heir might mean to lose her, not necessarily, but the probabilities were that way.

It was not a situation to bring out the best that was in a man. Such a rivalry with one's own relations is apt to develop the sneak, the time-server, the hypocrite. One must seek to please at the cost of inclination, thus breeding insincerity, and sometimes hatred where one must seem to love; for nature does not like to be forced, and has a way of striking balances. There was once a slave who kept in a secret place an effigy of his master, upon which he returned with interest and satisfaction all the kicks and cuffs his master had bestowed upon him. An old Voodoo woman had told him that his master would feel them all.

Philippe had preserved, under temptation, a fine integrity. Desiring above all things to marry Joséphine, he sought to be worthy of her. And if, for the same reason, he tried to please his uncle, it was no effort, because he acknowledged a debt of gratitude to him for many things.

"I owe him all I am and all I have," he said to himself, with simple loyalty. "He is my uncle and the head of our family, and I could do no less than love him."

He felt sure that his uncle appreciated his devotion, which was in marked contrast to the obsequious sycophancy of several of the other nephews. He was not energetic, Philippe was not; he could perhaps keep what he had, but was not likely to add to it greatly by his own exertions. He would make an ideal heir for a rich man.

Joséphine had kept him at arm's length for a long time.

"You should love me, Joséphine," he would say, "as I love you."

"But imagine," she would reply, "that you should not be the heir, in what a predicament I should be placed! Loving you, I should be compelled to wed another. You would not wish me such a fate?"

No, he would not. He could not think of Joséphine as another's, without a shudder.

"Perish the thought!" he cried. "I should run away with you."

"No, Philippe, you could not. The church would not approve."

"I would marry you *à l'Americain,* before a magistrate."

"No, Philippe, I could not marry without the blessing of the church, nor without my father's consent."

Don José did nothing to interfere with their friendship. He thought of it as nothing more than a childish fancy which would yield to the serious exigencies of life. Moreover, Philippe might be the heir—his friend Pierre had always spoken kindly of Philippe. Again, Philippe had no entanglements of the heart to interfere with Joséphine's happiness. If he should be the heir, he might take Joséphine with her father's blessing. If not, she would do her duty. She was too desirable for any but the best; and there were other reasons, powerful ones, which must constrain her.

Philippe thought he had good grounds for his elation as he rode along the way to Trois Pigeons. Only the day before, his uncle had sent for him and had asked for an estimate of his debts. He was, by the way, a real estate broker and dealer.

"I do not owe a picayune which is not amply secured, Uncle Pierre," he had answered, "except my tailor's bill, and that can wait."

His uncle had seemed surprised.

"Your business would pay better with more capital invested," he said. "I will lend you twenty thousand dollars. Put it in houses. The city is growing. In two years you will have doubled it. You may give me your note for the money. But say nothing to the others about it. You are the only one that deserves it."

Philippe had accepted the proffered loan, regarding it and his uncle's commendation, as an earnest of his heirship; and he was now on his way to Trois Pigeons with joy in his heart and a song upon his lips, to impart his momentous secret to Joséphine.

As Philippe drew near enough to see the belvedere of Trois Pigeons rising above the tree-tops, he came face to face with a strange cavalcade. Not so strange either, indeed, but striking. A giant, deeply pock-marked Negro and a one-eyed mulatto, shackled together, wrist to wrist and ankle to ankle, so that they must move as one man, were stumbling along the road, and behind them came, on horseback, a white man by courtesy, long of hair, swarthy of skin, high of cheek bone, with a huge sombrero on his head, a pistol at his belt, and in his hand a rawhide whip. It was Mendoza, the half-breed Spanish-Indian overseer of Don José Morales.

"Good day, M. Beaurepas," said the overseer with a wave of the hand.

"Good day, Mendoza. Who are these scurvy rascals?"

"Hist! M. Philippe, say nothing at the house. They are masterless men—runaways. I found them on the plantation. Señor Morales ordered them whipped, and then would have let them go."

"We are free men," protested the mulatto. "Our boat

was overturned in the river and we sought refuge on the bank. One would not treat a dog so."

"Silence, brute," said the overseer, with a slash of the whip which left an angry welt across the speaker's face. "They have no free papers," he went on. "My salary is a year behind. I shall turn them over the authorities. If they cannot prove their freedom, they will be sold as vagrants and my share of the money will pay me up."

It was a lawful thing. Runaway slaves were dangerous to society. A Negro without proof of his freedom was presumed to be a runaway slave. Philippe glanced at the two manacled men. They were desperate-looking fellows, the mulatto seeming even fiercer than the black, as he glowered at the two white men with his one menacing eye, like a chained tiger.

"Ah, well, Mendoza, I wish you good luck. It is well you have them shackled, or they would murder you before you reached the city."

"Never fear, Monsieur Philippe. It is my trade to manage such cattle. You will find the señora at home."

Philippe rode on until he entered the gate of Trois Pigeons, and dismounted in the *patio*. A Negro lad sprang forward and took charge of his horse. A colored girl standing on the verandah, darted into the house to warn her mistress. The house servants all loved their young mistress and took a personal interest in her love affair, with the conditional character of which they were all familiar.

As Philippe set foot upon the verandah, Joséphine came forward to meet him—a Southern beauty, moving with an unconscious, undulatory grace. Her gown of dotted white muslin was made in the Empire style, low in the neck, with short sleeves, clearly defining, above the high waist line, the youthful curve of her well-formed bosom. She wore this free costume with virginal modesty, though her arms were bare, and her somewhat worn red morocco *mules* nursed the soft white skin of her little feet with no jealous stocking to intervene. Of the pure Spanish type, she might have stepped direct from a Goya canvas. The broad low brow of her little head was crowned with a wealth of dark hair, which she had washed that morning, and which, gathered loosely with a red ribbon, fell in a dusky flood far below her waist.

From the clear olive of her face, to which the excitement of Philippe's visit had lent a dash of a richer color, her large dark eyes, shaded by long lashes over which her arched eyebrows nearly met, flashed welcome to her lover as she held forth a hand which showed, as clearly as a human hand could show, that none of her ancestors had ever done any work.

"Welcome, Philippe," she said, with shy warmth.

"Good day, Joséphine. Is your father at home?"

"No, Philippe, he is at the far end of the plantation. Will you ride out to him?"

"No, Joséphine, I will wait."

"Shall I send a Negro for him?"

"No, Joséphine. I would not disturb him. It is you I came to see."

Joséphine sighed a sigh of contentment. They went into the cool, high-ceilinged hall. They were alone, except for the servants about the house. Her duenna, an elderly cousin of her father who made her home with them, was taking her siesta in the adjoining room, but she was a hard sleeper. Philippe told Joséphine of his uncle's generosity, and of his own convictions.

"Is it not clear, Joséphine, that I shall be the heir?"

"There can be no doubt of it, Philippe. You are the best of them all, and your uncle has perceived it, and has chosen this way to indicate his preference. He does not make his choice known to the others, because he is an old man, and would end his days in peace."

"Then, Joséphine," cried Philippe, "there is no reason why you should not love me."

"N-o, Philippe, I suppose—"

She had not time to finish, for he closed her lips with a kiss. They were seated side by side on the faded Louis Quinze settee. He was reaching for another kiss, when a sudden barking of dogs and scurrying of Negro children in the yard, announced an important arrival.

"It is papa," said Joséphine, starting to her feet. "I'll go and meet him."

Old Don José shook hands with Philippe. He listened with grave interest to Philippe's story.

"It is a good sign," he said. "You have substantial ground for hope. How is he?"

"Feeble in health, but bright and keen in mind. Since there is no doubt, Señor Morales, there can be no objections to my coming oftener?"

"Patience, Philippe, patience! He has not named the heir—the cup has not yet reached the lip. Joséphine is young and must not be bound by a betrothal, nor would I have her affections too deeply involved. When my friend Pierre announces that you are to be his heir, you may have her with my blessing. Until then, you may see her once a month, Philippe, once a month. Wait, and hope!"

Philippe went away disconsolate. Once a month! Well, he would see her oftener than that!

She came to town now and then to hear mass or to shop, in company with her duenna or a servant, and he would set a

Negro lad to watch the Natchez Road and notify him whenever Mademoiselle Morales came to town.

V.

THE QUADROON BALL

Though Louisiana had been part of the American Republic for nearly twenty years, the historic visit of a French duke to New Orleans which took place at about this period, was an event of tremendous social importance. The spiritual nexus which bound the Creoles to the land of their forefathers had been modified but not destroyed by the change of political dominion. The echoes of the French Revolution still resounded loudly in New Orleans, although its watchword of "Liberty, Equality and Fraternity," no more harmonized with slavery and the Code Noir than did the Declaration of Independence, and the fall of the Bastille still continued to be celebrated.

As a matter of fact Louisiana had never been a free commonwealth until 1808, when it became a state of the Union. The bureaucratic monarchy of Louis XV, which from a distance of four thousand miles regulated every petty detail of government, had been succeeded by a Spanish despotism really less meddlesome, but seemingly more oppressive because of the lack of sympathy between rulers and ruled. Upon its formal return to France in 1803, the colony had been sold by Napoleon, without consulting the inhabitants, for a ridiculously small sum, to the United States, and the political status of the former province became and continued to be for several years after the American annexation that of a territory. The only spark of independence in the history of the city had been the futile resistance made to the transfer of the colony to Spain in 1768, and this momentary self-assertion had been so severely punished that it was never repeated. The American occupation had been received with protests loud and deep, but without active hostility. French by blood and temperament, and for thirty years the sole remnant of the French colonies in North America, Louisiana,—for as Paris was France, so New Orleans was Louisiana,—clung tenaciously to the language of France—of Bienville and Frontenac, of all the pioneers who had covered the history of New France with glory,—and held fast to the Catholic faith and to the traditions of the mother country. Reflecting, sentimentally, the political movements of France, the Creoles had shared the glory of Napoleon, and though no longer French politically, had cheered the restoration of the monarchy. So that, even as late as 1820, the visit of a royal duke of the restored dynasty was something more than a social event; it struck a slumbering chord of loyalty to race and caste, which neither conquest nor purchase had destroyed.

New Orleans, therefore, had exerted itself to entertain fittingly the Duc de Nemours. There were dinners, fêtes and balls galore; there were discreet *petits soupers,* and *parties carrées;* for the duke was a gay young blade and French to the core; some years of exile in England had been only partly compensated by a very lively career after the restoration. A desire to see the world, as well as the wish to escape from an embarrassing entanglement, had brought his royal highness to America and to New Orleans. As a stranger, the duke was interested in objects of local interest, and was introduced to all the pleasure of the town. The lottery held a special drawing during his visit. The gaming houses on Canal and Carondelet Streets, upon which his highness looked in now and then, were much frequented by those who wished to see a duke play at cards or roulette. There was an extra season of opera, a grand ball for the social *élite* of the city, and on another night of the same week, a quadroon ball of unparalleled splendor.

This institution, for many years a feature of New Orleans life, was an outgrowth of the exotic civilization of a pioneer race, who, bringing with them no wives, before the advent of women of their own race had mated, more or less like the birds, with the Indian and Negro women. Though frequently severe and even cruel slaveholders, the Latins have nevertheless always shown a marked affinity for the darker races, for whom they had never the harsh Anglo-Saxon contempt. Recognizing their own blood, too, even when mingled with that of slaves, it had always been the fashion in Latin America to manumit the children of these left-handed unions, and to provide for their support. There had thus grown up in New Orleans the large class of free colored people known as the quadroon caste, of which Paul and Julie Marchand were members, the women of which, say the chroniclers of those days, vied with the white Creole women in beauty, in dress, and in graceful dancing. And the quadroon women were the reason for the quadroon ball.

The quadroon ball was held on Thursday night, following the grand ball on Wednesday night. The presence of a royal duke was as exciting an event to the frail tinted beauties of the French quarter as to the paler ladies of the aristocracy. Every staid quadroon, long since retired upon a legacy or a pension, wished to be present; every young girl with a future yet to be provided for, fluttered with excitement at the prospect of meeting, in a scene of brilliant gaiety, a royal duke of France. Their life—poor butterflies of passion! poor hostages for the chastity of their white sisters!—their life yet had its compensations. They gained freedom, ease, sometimes a love, which, whatever it may have lacked of the romantic devotion which goes by that name, preserved them from the pains of poverty and brought to their children beauty and brains and sometimes wealth. It brought, too, the quadroon ball, boxes at the opera, a veneer of courtesy, under which lurked, of course, the brutality inseparable from slavery and all its incidents, but it spread a fair covering of flowers over the morass, and one might, if one chose, shut one's eyes to the spots where the cloak was thin or the slough laid bare.

The quadroon ball was, of course, for white gentlemen only. No amount of wealth or education could qualify a male quadroon for this gathering of the cream of his own womanhood. They were meat for his masters. Meekness and self-effacement were the price which the quadroon man paid for the privilege of living and doing business in New Orleans. If he could find a wife among the younger quadroon women, all well and good, but if she were personally attractive he did well to keep her in seclusion. If he were not so fortunate, he might hire or buy a black or colored housekeeper, or perhaps marry the endowed mistress of some white man who had tired of her when her cheeks began to fade or her eyes to lose their luster. For the wealthier quadroons were themselves sometimes the owners of slaves. With most of them the love of liberty, like that of their betters, was mainly personal. If

married her before she had scarcely come into contact with the outer world. Her sister Lizette had been as carefully brought up, but a touch of waywardness had made her chafe under conventional restraints. Vain, frivolous, beautiful in the quadroon way, the blood of the gay Creole gentlemen and their dusky sweethearts throbbed in her veins in a ceaseless demand for excitement, gaiety, pleasure. Marchand had planned to take her with his wife and children to France, and there, with the money her father had left her, to marry her to some gentleman to whom, with Gallic liberality, the bar sinister and the dash of African blood would not outweigh an ample dowry. If, however, there should be any added disability to overcome, the task would be by that much the more difficult. Even the most liberal of decent Frenchmen was likely to demand the elementary virtue in a wife. For an unmarried young woman to attend the quadroon ball was, to all intents and purposes, by the social code of New Orleans, a bid for the protection, without the marriage ceremony, of some gentleman who could afford such a luxury. Paris was not so far from New Orleans but that many people of the latter city, both white and colored, were often in the French capital. While a student there, Marchand had formed a wide acquaintance among the younger men of the city. He had met, in one or two gay parties, this very duke whose visit was the occasion of this very ball; the duke had perhaps forgotten him, nor would he wish to recall himself to his remembrance. In Paris they had met upon the sort of equality upon which gentlemen everywhere meet in public places. He had even engaged in a fencing bout with his highness once, in a Parisian *salle d'armes* where Marchand was conspicuous for his skill with the foils. If they should meet in New Orleans it would have to be upon a very different footing, and he therefore preferred that they should not meet at all. Lizette at the ball, with her very striking beauty, would be sure to attract attention, with the attendant advertisement, and the consequent reflection upon his own family.

"She has been very restless and excited," said Julie. "She has wondered what a royal duke was like, and was telling me only today of Madame Claudine's entrancing description of the quadroon balls. I fear, Paul, that she has gone there."

"Let me see," said Paul, "the ball begins at eight. I shall go at once and fetch her home."

"You'll not be admitted," said his wife.

"It's a masked ball," replied Paul. "I'll wear a domino. If I can but get her ear, I shall bring her away. She will hardly have arrived."

"You'll run the risk of insult if you go."

"We shall run the risk of dishonor if I don't."

Julie, after a brief search, found a black domino, or half-mask, and Marchand, having thrust it into his pocket, hastened down Carondelet Street to the corner of Condé and soon reached the building, later occupied by a convent of colored nuns, but in this earlier generation devoted to scenes of pleasure in which the quadroon and octoroon women of that age played anything but a conventual role. The front was brilliantly lighted. As Marchand approached, a lemon-tinted, deep-bosomed young woman, in an elaborate ball gown, satin slippers, a light wrap thrown across her bare shoulders, was entering the hall on the arm of the son of the mayor of New Orleans. Marchand stood for a moment and watched them pass through the lighted portal, in which stood a very tall mulatto in gorgeous livery,—black men were not allowed at the quadroon balls in any capacity, under pain of death, though they might light the way of the women thither with lanterns. It was a small city, and carriages were seldom used in going to balls of any kind.

As Marchand, having put on his mask, approached the door and was about to enter it, the porter, touching his cap respectfully, barred the way.

"Pardon, Miché, but your ticket?"

Marchand ran his hand through his pockets as though searching for his ticket, but of course found nothing, since he had no ticket.

"I've evidently left it behind," he replied, with an air of annoyance.

"Then your name, Miché, if you please?"

Marchand hesitated, but for a moment only. Slipping his hand into his pocket, he drew forth a gold piece which he slipped into the doorman's hand.

"I wish to preserve my incognito," he murmurred. "It is all right; I belong to the duke's suite."

The doorkeeper in turn hesitated, but the bribe was a large one, and the visitor was undoubtedly a gentleman.

"Enter, Miché, and a thousand thanks for your generosity. Miché le Duc is just ahead of you."

Marchand mounted the stairs hastily. He had dressed himself before leaving home, in the costume of the period, which was a copy, not more than a year behind, of that of the Paris court and salon. The elegance of his attire, the clear olive of his complexion, so far as it was visible around the small black mask, in contrast with the straight, dark brown hair which fell to his shoulders; his slender but sinewy hand, with the nails carefully trimmed and polished and bearing several rings set with precious stones, made up a *tout ensemble* which no one would have suspected as belonging to other than a gentleman of the first social rank. Absorbed in his quest and protected from recognition by his mask, Marchand moved freely among the gathering throng.

The scene was a brilliant one. The large ballroom, profusely decorated with cut flowers and potted palms, was lighted by a grand chandelier with dozens of wax candles and crystal pendants shivering with the vibration of the dance, and flashing with all the colors of the spectrum. The floor was of solid oak, three inches thick, said to be the best dancing floor in New Orleans. Most of the women were young and shapely, many of them not casually distinguishable from white, and the men, also for the most part young, were of the cream of New Orleans society. A mulatto orchestra was playing Gottschalk's *Danse Nègre*, replete with the languorous tropical charm of Creole melody. The ball was not yet in full swing, but a few couples were moving over the polished floor to the rhythm of the music.

Marchand threw a hasty glance around the ballroom but did not discover the object of his search. But in one corner, in vivacious conversation with a well-known merchant with whom he himself had dealings, he recognized, under her mask, the sprightly Madame Claudine, the fashionable quadroon *modiste* of the Rue Carondelet, the full battery of whose sparkling eyes and full-blown charms, set off by one of the famous gowns of her own make with which she clothed the *élégantes* of New Orleans, was in active operation. Costly diamonds sparkled in her ears, and she toyed with a fan which had belonged to Marie Antoinette. For Claudine was rich and went every two years to Paris to bring back the latest fashions. It was the dream of her life to live in that city and conduct a pension for colonial gentlemen.

Marchand started toward her and had covered more than half the distance between them, when he hesitated. That Lizette was at the ball he had no doubt, but was it desirable for him to make his presence known to Madame Claudine? It was not at all necessary for her to know that he had attended the quadroon ball—it was serious breach of caste, which if known, could do him no good. If Claudine should be indiscreet enough to mention if afterwards, it might still further complicate a situation which he was beginning to find well-nigh intolerable.

Through the long French windows he could see the couples promenading in the broad gallery which ran alongside the ballroom, where a dance might be sat out or whispered flirtation carried on. Marchand moved toward the nearest window. It was necessary, in order to reach it, to pass a group of gentlemen who stood engaged in animated conversation. In one of these Marchand recognized the young duke, who, as the guest of the evening, was unmasked, and he recognized, with the keen memory of hatred, the voice of the gentleman who was addressing the duke.

"We shall unmask in ten minutes. It is unfair to deprive your highness any longer of the full splendor of these charms. I will give the signal at nine o'clock on the minute; those who come in costume will have arrived by that hour—if not, it is their own fault."

"I saw just now," returned the duke, "a girl who struck my fancy. She was gowned in pale yellow and had the figure of a Hebe in miniature. I shall be glad to see her face, I'm sure it will be in keeping. There she goes now," he added, nodding toward the opposite side of the room.

Marchand's eyes followed those of the duke, and rested upon Lizette, who was at that moment entering the room by another door. She was masked, but he could not have mistaken her anywhere. He had seen the stuff of which her gown was made; he himself had made her a Christmas present of the necklace she wore, and she walked with a seductive grace that bordered unconsciously upon wantonness.

"I'll introduce your highness as soon as we unmask," said Henri Beaurepas, whom Marchand had recognized in the speaker. "Perhaps we need not wait. She is at present unattended, and you may not be allowed a monopoly after she unmasks. She will likely prove a pleasant acquaintance and worth following up. I have designs of my own in that quarter, but will yield precedence to a distinguished guest—whose visit is a short one!" he concluded with a significant laugh.

Marchand darted before them and moved swiftly through the crowd toward Lizette. He wished by all means to prevent her unmasking at the ball. He expected to sail for France in a few weeks and take the girl with him. In a country where their origin entailed no insurmountable social disabilities, and with means and education which would gain them admission to good social circles, it was not at all unlikely that the Duc de Nemours, an aristocrat with democratic tastes might come face to face, in some Paris ball-room, with Lizette. The manners and morals of Europe were none too strict a century ago, but respectable women did not attend the students' balls in the Latin Quarter nor the more brilliant assemblies of the demimonde, to which the quadroon balls of New Orleans could only be compared. It was important therefore, that Marchand should reach his sister-in-law and get her away from the ball unnoticed before the moment for unmasking.

His movements, however, had not been unobserved. Henri Beaurepas had noticed the start with which the man in the black domino had paused beside his own group and had observed the rapid movement of Marchand toward the corner where Lizette was seated. Excusing himself for a moment, he left the duke in conversation with the third member of his party and followed Marchand quickly across the room, in time to hear him address the young woman.

"Lizette," he said sternly, "you must come away immediately. You should not be here. The signal for unmasking will be given in three minutes. If you're not away by then, your good name will be ruined and our family disgraced."

Lizette had started guiltily. She knew she was in the wrong, and did not stop to argue.

"I'll get my cloak," she said, rising at once and moving toward the cloak-room.

Henri Beaurepas had overheard the colloquy and had recognized the speaker. Quadroon men were not allowed at the *cordon bleu* balls. This intruder had broken caste. A man of finer fiber might have recognized the provocation and have helped rather than hindered a praiseworthy action. But Henri Beaurepas was not a man of fine fiber. Not only had he promised the duke an introduction to this tropical butterfly, but beneath her mask he had recognized the young girl who only a few days before had cast him a most coquettish glance from Claudine's front window in Carondelet Street. This was a golden opportunity, which he by no means wished to forfeit. He would like, too, to punish the insolence of this quadroon, who had more than once, in other places, assumed to exercise the privileges of white gentlemen. There must be some way to get rid of him, and at the same time prevent scandal which might mar the harmony of the occasion.

"I have it," he said to himself with a gesture of satisfaction. Turning to the dancers behind him, he touched one and then another upon the shoulder, and in a moment had a little group of four or five young men around him, among them his brother Hector. He whispered to them certain instructions, and they moved off toward the entrance.

Meantime Lizette had donned her cloak and came toward Marchand, who tendered his arm and started toward the doorway. As they approached the main entrance a liveried servant came forward and said in Negro French:

"If monsieur will permit me, gentlemen and ladies wishing to leave the ball-room can pass out unobserved by the side entrance."

He motioned toward a door at the side. As they approached it, several gentlemen converged upon them as if by accident, Marchand was separated from Lizette, and a moment later found himself upon the other side of the door, which was closed between them. At the same moment his arm was grasped upon either side. As, taken utterly by surprise, he struggled to free himself and struck out with blind indignation, he suffered some violence in return and received a blow upon the head which stretched him senseless on the pavement.

VI.

In the Calabozo

When Marchand recovered consciousness he found himself lying on a rough bed in the Calabozo, or city prison. What hour of the night it was he did not know, for the prison was shrouded in darkness, except for the dim light of a lantern which but faintly illuminated the corridor, so that he was unable to consult his watch.

The quadroon men were, as a rule, of amiable disposition and cheerful temperament. While they regarded their social treatment as cruel and unjust, and discussed it among themselves with much animation, the cruelty was mainly a matter of feeling and might be ignored by the philosophical; and to the injustice, consisting for the most part of things denied instead of things taken away, they were at least accustomed, with the callousness which custom engenders. While regarded as inferior to the whites, they were looked upon and treated as much superior to the darker people. One of the principal streets of the city was named after a free woman of color, who owned the land through which it was opened. This discrimination in their favor was also, to one not a philosopher, a source of comfort. Whether or not the Creole quadroons were a philosophic race was not really important, since the pleasure-loving French temperament, superimposed upon the easy-going African, produced a usually placid acceptance of the situation which had all the effect of philosophy.

In this respect, however, Paul Marchand differed from the average quadroon. Whether it was the fiery spirit of some adventurous European ancestor, or the blood of some African chief who had exercised the power of life and death before being broken to the hoe, or whether the free air of revolutionary France had wrought upon him—whatever the reason, he had chafed more than most under the restrictions of his caste.

When the restraints and humiliations to which he was subjected had culminated in his rude arrest and ruder imprisonment, is it to be wondered that his bosom was filled with stormy feelings which found a poor vent in pacing up and down the narrow cell, and impotent shaking of his fists and trilling the r's of picturesque French oaths? For despite any reputed strain of alien blood, Paul Marchand was French to the finger-tips; no Creole of Louisiana was truer to type.

When he had worked off his first paroxysm of rage, he began to consider his predicament. It was a matter for serious thought. His position was an awkward one. In the altercation at the ballroom he had struck several white men, among them Hector Beaurepas. Under the *code noir*, for a man of color to strike a white man was to render himself liable, before the law, if he escaped immediate death at the hands of the person struck, to fine, imprisonment, whipping, or, in an aggravated case, the loss of the hand which had struck the blow. Obviously he would need a good lawyer, and it would be well to summon him at once. He ought also to send a message to his wife, apprizing her of his whereabouts.

Marchand raised his voice and called for a jailer. There was no response. He called again more loudly and shook the iron bars of the cell door. There was still no response, but from the adjoining cell came a Spanish oath, and a gruff voice, demanding, in Gumbo French, why he was making such an infernal racket in the middle of the night, when honest and respectable prisoners were trying to sleep. Finding it impossible to secure the attention of a jailer, Marchand made the best of the situation, composed himself upon the layer of foul straw spread on the floor in lieu of a bed, and joined the ranks of the honest and peaceable prisoners who sought forgetfulness of their troubles in slumber.

He had slept he did not know how long, when gradually there stole upon his senses the sounds of a whispered conversation, and as he slowly returned to consciousness he discovered that these sounds came from the cell adjoining his own. Whether the mortar had fallen out from between the stones of the old partition wall, or whether, in the stillness of midnight, his ear was attuned to just the pitch that would catch, through the barred front of his own cell, the whispered words which sounded from the one adjoining, in any event the conversation was distinctly audible.

"It is an outrage," said an unctuous Negro voice. "We have done nothing; they had no means of knowing that we intended to do anything. We were beaten without mercy; we were thrown into prison; we are to be sold into slavery, because, forsooth, we cannot prove that we are free men!"

"We shall have revenge," returned a harsher voice, which to Marchand sounded vaguely familiar. "I hate them all, root and branch. I would kill the last one, even as our people did in San Domingo. Yet it is a large contract, and we might ourselves be killed in the process."

"True," replied the other, "but we need not attempt so much. They have all injured us, but not all equally. If we can avenge ourselves upon those who whipped us and sent us here, it would be at least something on account."

The conversation proceeded for a quarter of an hour. Once a rat scurrying across the floor from some unoccupied cell caused them to be silent for a few minutes. Reassured that they were not being overheard, they resumed their conversation, which took the form of a plot to burn down a certain plantation house, west of the city, to cut the levee and flood the plantation, and to poison the cattle and horses in the stables.

Marchand listened with instinctive interest. Himself the proprietor, through his wife, of several houses and a plantation, the destruction of property appealed to him as to any other land owner. He listened intently and finally gathered from their description of it, that the place marked for destruction was the house of old Don José Morales, five miles from the city, along the Natchez Road.

Negro insurrections were ever the nightmare of slavery. They rarely occurred, but were always feared—conscience makes cowards of us all. Under the strict repressive discipline of the pioneer French and Spanish slave-holders, such few risings as had ever been attempted, were small and easily suppressed, and the single one which took place in Louisiana after the American occupation, had proved a costly failure for the rioters. Nevertheless, the awful example of San Domingo, where the land, for its sins, had been drenched in blood, was always before the eyes of those just across the Gulf of Mexico who still fostered the institution of slavery.

Under other circumstances Marchand would have been deeply impressed and indeed shocked by this conversation, and would have felt it his duty to warn the authorities and denounce the conspirators. But his recent experiences had drawn him for the moment away from his quadroon leaning toward the whites and aloofness from the blacks, and left him in the camp of the latter. They, too, had suffered; they, too, had been wronged; they, too, were entitled to compensation, if only by way of revenge. He did not know this Don José Morales except by sight, and by reputation as the proudest of the old Spanish Creoles, with very poor credit commercially, and with a daughter whose beauty was the talk of the town. But he was a white man, and for this night all white men were Paul Marchand's enemies; what should happen to them was no concern of his. They were all his enemies. If he could make them change places with himself, or with the two degraded Negroes in the adjoining cell, he would do it with a holy joy. Perhaps, he thought, after a while, he might make a few exceptions, but only a few. He fell asleep again.

He awoke a while later, when everything was still, except for the stertorous snore of one of his neighbors and the shrill chirp of a cricket in the wall. Sleep having had a calming effect upon his passion, the seriousness of his own predicament, should Hector Beaurepas prove vindictive, was even more apparent; and it occurred to Marchand that in this event his knowledge of the contemplated plot might be utilized to his advantage. To reveal a Negro plot was a public service almost great enough to counter-balance any misdemeanor. That he could escape a fine Marchand did not expect; imprisonment was not unlikely; but he would consider himself fortunate if he escaped any more ignominious punishment, and he would do much to accomplish this. But even this course would not be entirely satisfying. The two prisoners, like himself, were martyrs to caste; whatever their characters or their crimes, it was not for these that they were incarcerated, but for the unpardonable and unescapable crime of color. To denounce them would be to condemn to certain death two men who might never have either opportunity or courage to execute their plans.

The rest of Marchand's night was spent in a fitful doze, through which the dawn seemed long in coming.

VII.

Monsieur Renard

In the morning Marchand sent for his lawyer. While, under the old regime in Louisiana, as under the system in the more northern states, the law provided that a man charged with a crime or misdemeanor should have a speedy trial, the accused was in fact brought to bar when it suited the convenience of the judge, the prosecuting attorney, or others who might be interested in the outcome. The wishes of the prisoner were the last to be consulted. Moreover, the French system regarded solitude, with its opportunities for reflection and meditation, as an excellent thing for a prisoner. The Americans had introduced trial by jury and other innovations, but they had not changed the Creole habit of mind. Being a man of color, with an influential white man interested against him, Marchand realized therefore, that he might be kept in prison for weeks without trial, and that it behooved him to secure, as soon as possible, the intervention of an equally influential white man in his own behalf.

The lawyer for whom Marchand very wisely sent was the same M. Jules Renard who had provided for his youth.

M. Renard's trust had long since terminated—at least Marchand had never called on him for funds since his marriage. But by habit he had always gone to M. Renard for legal advice and service in his business affairs and in the management of his wife's property. A good lawyer, M. Renard would no doubt have sufficient interest in the welfare of a profitable client to make it reasonably certain that he would do everything possible to extricate Marchand from his unpleasant predicament. That it was a matter for influence rather than legal procedure Marchand knew quite well. It might be possible to use money, if necessary and if the bribe were large enough. Henri Beaurepas was a notorious spendthrift, in whom, in case he were obdurate, a sum of money large enough might promote magnanimity.

A piece of silver in the palm of a turnkey brought M. Renard to the prison early in the morning—so early, indeed, that Marchand himself wondered that a lawyer of M. Renard's standing should trouble himself to attend any client at such an hour. But the motives which influence human conduct are not always visible upon the surface of things, as Marchand was soon to learn concerning others than his lawyer.

M. Renard was admitted to the prisoner's cell. He stepped forward towards Marchand with both hands extended, exclaiming with unction, as he advanced—

"My dear fellow, this is an outrage! For what can you possibly have been shut up here? It is some mistake. I shall see the magistrate at once."

Marchand wondered at the warmth of his lawyer's greeting. In their former intercourse M. Renard had been always courteous. Your true Creole gentleman was ever the pink of courtesy. He graded his politeness, of course, according to the degree of its object, with a due regard to social distinctions. A wealthy colored client was not a person to be treated otherwise than with consideration. Nevertheless, the courtesy shown to a quadroon, no matter how deserving, was not quite that exhibited toward one of the ruling class who possessed equal claims for consideration. For instance, in their former intercourse, M. Renard had addressed his client as "Marchand" or sometimes "Monsieur Marchand," the latter itself a distinct concession. Upon this occasion he had accosted him familiarly, but Marchand was quite man of the world enough to know that this betokened no falling off of respect; indeed it was this very fact, combined with a certain air of sympathy which he had never before observed in his lawyer, but of which he was immediately conscious, that had made him wonder.

He briefly related the incidents of the evening, including of course his visit to the quadroon ball and the reasons for it. M. Renard was elderly and discreet, and would respect the seal of professional confidence. Moreover, the freemasonry of feeling which the lawyer had manifested bred in Marchand a corresponding expansiveness.

"It was a mistake, my dear Paul, a grave mistake," declared M. Renard, with either a real or a well-simulated indignation. "It shall be repaired immediately, and with due satisfaction to your honor. I'll see the magistrate at once."

M. Renard went away, leaving Marchand all the more puzzled. The honor of a quadroon might indeed be a very vital thing, to the quadroon, but it was not usual for white men, however amiable, to concern themselves about something which theoretically could not exist. Under the old regime, when every white man was a walking arsenal, men of color were not allowed to bear arms, and Marchand himself, had he carried upon his person when arrested a sword or pistol or dagger, would have been liable to a severe fine, because of that fact alone. An honor which, in an age of dueling, could not be defended with sword or pistol, was not a thing to be seriously considered. Hence Marchand's anger took secondary place to the perplexity into which his lawyer's conduct had thrown him. Not only was he addressed in terms of friendly warmth by a leading citizen, but credited with and promised satisfaction for an honor which, in his experience, white men had arrogated to themselves as their exclusive privilege.

What M. Renard said to the magistrate is not of record, though the tenor of it may be inferred from subsequent events. At all events it proved sufficient to obtain the prisoner's release, and Marchand, somewhat ruffled in spirit as well as clothing, though his feelings had been slightly soothed by the promptness of his release and the championship of his lawyer, returned to the bosom of his family.

His wife greeted him with an affection well nigh hysterical. She was a beautiful woman, dark-eyed, *petite*, on whom the slight strain of African blood left its mark more in a certain softness and pensiveness of expression than in any pronounced negroid feature. After Marchand had embraced and kissed his wife, he snatched up their youngest child, a baby girl of two, who threw her tiny arms around his neck and cooed with infantile delight, while little Celestine clung to his knees and clamorously demanded her share of attention.

"We did not sleep at all last night," said Julie. "We were in deep distress, not knowing what had happened to you, and fearing the worst, until M. Renard sent word to us an hour ago that you were safe and would soon be here. About ten o'clock old Terence, M. Pierre Beaurepas's butler, came to the house and said his master wished to see you immediately, upon a matter of grave importance. But you were not at home nor could I tell him where you were."

"I can't imagine what business he could have with us,"

said Paul. "And no matter. If it was for anything concerning my interest, it can wait. If it concerned his own, he may thank his precious nephews. At what hour did Lizette reach home?"

"Immediately after you were separated," returned Julie. "When you had been taken away, M. Hector Beaurepas came up with the Duc de Nemours, and the signal having been given, would have had her unmask. Frightened by what you had said, she implored him to desist. On the contrary he insisted. M. Philippe Beaurepas joined them, and having inquired concerning the affair, demanded that she be permitted to depart without unmasking. The duke was appealed to as arbitrator. As became a gallant gentleman, he decided in favor of Lizette, and M. Philippe gave her his arm to the street and sent his own servant home with her, without having seen her face or learned her name."

"It is all the same," said Marchand. "Her name will be all over New Orleans before night."

"But not at all," said Julie. "She dismissed the servant a block from here and came the rest of the way alone. She was not molested, and no one knows of her escapade except Madame Claudine and ourselves. Claudine will say nothing; she has done wrong and she knows it, and would fear to lose a valuable client."

"I hope she'll be silent," said Marchand. "As for Mademoiselle Lizette, we shall keep her under lock and key until we sail for France, which will be within a few weeks. The air of New Orleans stifles me. I am a man—a free man and not a slave—and I must breathe the air of a free country. I hate these *sacré* whites!"

"They are not all unkind," returned Julie. "My father was white, and he left me his property. And M. Philippe Beaurepas—"

"They are merely the exceptions which prove the rule," returned Paul. "They despise us, and I hate them all, each according to his own degree of scorn. Your father was kind in a way, yes, he gave you his name and his fortune. As for mine, I have not been permitted even to know who he was. I hate them all, and I feel that I shall have my revenge for the slights they have put upon me, I do not know when or how, but that sometime, somehow, I shall have it."

The excited manner in which Marchand had spoken, so impressed the little Bébé that with eyes big with apprehension she hid herself within the folds of her mother's skirt and peeped out affrightedly at this strangely fierce papa, so different from the kinder one who dandled her on his knee and fed her with bon-bons.

VIII.

The Will

New Orleans society has resumed its wonted placidity, after the departure of the Duke of Nemours, which took place about a week after the quadroon ball given in his honor, when it was thrown into a state of even greater commotion by the will of old Pierre Beaurepas, the filing of which for probate was duly chronicled in *Le Moniteur de la Louisiane.* For this fine old Creole gentleman, having successfully stood off the common enemy from the outposts during a long siege of the gout, was at length compelled to capitulate when the disease attacked the citadel, his heart. His death, while a matter of much concern to a small group, had been expected and its effect upon the public therefore discounted. Nor was death so uncommon a thing in New Orleans—a city of malaria, yellow fever, and duels—as of itself to attract any particular remark. The disposition of the Beaurepas estate was, however, so entirely unlooked for as not only to bring consternation to a few but stupefaction to the whole community.

By this remarkable document neither Hector, nor Adolphe, nor Raoul, nor Henri, nor Philippe Beaurepas was made the heir or the beneficiary in any degree whatsoever. With the exception that freedom and small legacies were bequeathed to his household servants, the great bulk of the estate,—land, houses, slaves, ships, stocks, bonds, money, pictures, books and personal effects,—was devised to a man who had not hitherto been known as at all connected with the deceased; a man who had been reared as a quadroon, who had married into the despised caste and had, moreover, made himself obnoxious to many good people by intemperate speech, and a tendency to intrude where men of his reputed class were not allowed. By a codicil, executed shortly before the testator's decease, substantial bequests were made to the Catholic Church for the use of its schools, and to the city corporation to build a hospital.

Even this astounding disposition of the property, however, was not sufficient to account for all the interest excited by the Beaurepas will. It was no uncommon thing for a white Creole father to leave a colored child a substantial estate.

Had not Tony Lacroix, the well known *rentier,* inherited some fifty houses from his father, Colonel Aristide Lacroix? Had not a large part of the quadroon holdings of New Orleans real estate had this origin? Was not even the wealth of this pestilent quadroon, Marchand, a bequest to his wife from her white father? No, the lash on the whip of the Beaurepas will which stirred the pulses of New Orleans lay in this—that by the terms of his will Pierre Beaurepas recognized this person, hitherto known on the legal records of New Orleans as "Paul Marchand, f. m. c."—"free man of color"—as his legitimate son, declared that he was white of the pure blood, and requested that he assume his name and place as his father's heir and the head of the Beaurepas family!

There was, of course, an underlying romance. The air of old New Orleans was full of romance. The old world superimposed upon the new; the careless mingling of races, the flux and reflux of governments—these and a dozen other things had made the city a center of adventure which pulsed with romance. The will of Pierre Beaurepas did not recount the story, and since it did not at once become public property, the Creole imagination was given full play for the concoction of whatever series of imaginary events might account for so strange an outcome. For, while it was not unknown that a quadroon or octoroon should pass for white, and while it had happened in rare instances that a white child, for whom there was no way to account except with shame and disgrace, had been permitted to grow up as colored, yet there had never been any case so fully authenticated or involving a family of so high a standing.

Those to whom this astounding will came with the greatest shock were of course the five nephews of Pierre Beaurepas. Picture to yourself five young men, each of whom had built for himself, out of great expectations, a lofty pedestal, upon which he should shine; a tower of Babel, as it were, which should lift him above the floods of poverty or misfortune; and then imagine this lofty structure demolished by a single thunderbolt and its building left floundering in the ruins, dazed by the shock of the disaster. Or, imagine a man sailing across a placid stream toward a pleasant goal, and that a sudden squall should overturn his craft and leave him struggling in the rough waves. Only some such figure as this could possibly typify the state of mind into which the Beaurepas cousins were precipitated by this remarkable will of their uncle Pierre.

What unutterable disappointment was theirs; into what depths of temperamental despair they were plunged; what maledictions they called down upon the soul of their deceased relative; what sources of consolation they sought to take off the first edge of their disappointment, it would not be kind here to recount. The power of wealth is nowhere more manifest than when wielded by a dead hand. The will of their uncle Pierre, which, had it been in favor of any one of them would have created envy, jealousy and hatred in the others, operated by its totally unanticipated character to unite them for the time being by a common bond of sympathy.

The will had been in the possession of M. Renard, old M. Beaurepas's lawyer, who had announced that he would make its contents known to the relatives after the funeral. The cousins, with no suspicion of its contents, and masking their jealousy of one another for the time being, had jointly attended the obsequies, which were very imposing, the funeral taking place from the Cathedral on the *vieux carré*. Clad in deep mourning they had followed the mortal part of their dead relative to its last resting place in the old St. Louis

Cemetery, and seen it deposited in the family tomb. Each had manifested considerable self-restraint; for each, feeling himself certain to be the heir, would have been inclined to resent as presumption any apparent putting forward of themselves on the part of the others, but for a certain pity at the disappointment which his misguided relatives must shortly endure. Let them get what little comfort they might from their fleeting self-deception. The awakening would be more than cruel enough to offset it.

Upon the return from the cemetery, where the remains of Pierre Beaurepas had been literally "laid on the shelf," the five cousins, M. Renard, and in the background the servants of the household, all gathered in the grand salon of the family mansion, and there waited, surrounded by the portraits of four generations of Beaurepas, to hear what the dead voice of the family's latest representative should declare as to the disposition of the estate which these four generations had accumulated.

M. Renard read the fateful document. During the stupor which fell upon the listeners as the terms of the will were disclosed, and ere the storm which followed could break loose, the servants were dismissed, rejoicing at the freedom conferred upon them, and M. Renard continued.

"M. Paul Beaurepas, *ci-devant* Marchand," he said, "the heir of the deceased, feeling some delicacy about intruding so soon upon the grief of the family with which his connection has been so recently recognized, has requested me to act as his representative upon this occasion, and in his name therefore I take possession of this house and the effects of my late client."

When he had spoken, Terence, the butler, his face aglow with happiness—for by his master's will he had been made free in person and independent in means—stepped forward and handed his late master's keys to the lawyer.

Then the storm burst.

"It is infamous," said Hector Beaurepas, "that our uncle should leave the estate to a quadroon."

"Pardon, Monsieur," exclaimed M. Renard. "M. Paul Beaurepas, hitherto Marchand, is recognized by the will of my client, as white *pur sang*—of the pure blood. That he has been reared as a quadroon was a misfortune, for which my late client had an excellent excuse, but it does not impair the purity of the blood of M. Paul Beaurepas."

"We will not endure it," declared Raoul Beaurepas. "Our uncle shall not disinherit us for this bastard of his, be he white or yellow."

"Again I would remind you, Monsieur, that the will of your late uncle, whose remains we have but just now consigned to their last resting-place, distinctly describes my present client, Paul Beaurepas, as his legitimate son. And even though there were a technical point involved, bearing upon the question of his legitimacy, this act of recognition of itself establishes, by the civil law, which is the law of Louisiana, the legitimacy of M. Paul Beaurepas. Were he a quadroon, he could take under this will; were he a natural son this will would yet convey to him the property; but as the recognized legitimate or legitimated son of M. Beaurepas, he would inherit, will or no will; for the proofs of his birth are in my possession, and I am authorized, both by the deceased and by M. Paul Beaurepas, whom I represent, to make them known to all who could have any possible interest."

"We demand them," said Hector Beaurepas. "We wish to know by what preposterous fairy tale we are to be deprived of our inheritance."

M. Renard had a Frenchman's love for dramatic effect. He cleared his throat, and assuming a pose similar to that in which he addressed the court during his most glowing pleas, delivered himself as follows, while his hearers listened, at first with an angry incredulity which, as he proceeded, changed to the settled gloom of unwelcome conviction.

"When I say," said M. Renard, "that the romantic story which I am about to relate involved the good name of a lady, I do not mean thereby to imply any reflection whatever upon the spotless purity and delicate sense of honor which characterized this lady together with all the other ladies of Louisiana. Nothing could be farther from my thoughts, now would it be safe for me, in a company of Southern gentlemen, to cast any such aspersion upon the sex which we honor and admire. But, as the greatest of English poets has said,

> 'Be thou as chaste as ice, as pure as snow,
> Thou shalt not escape calumny;'

and no degree of foresight or discretion can always guard against accident or the unforeseen."

"For example, let us imagine a case. A lady, fresh from the convent, in the flower of youth, is married, without consulting her own wishes, to a man whom she has scarcely seen. Although her heart has been given to another, she stifles her feelings and in all wifely honor for years performs her duty to the man whose name she bears. But he is unworthy to possess such a treasure. He repays her devotion with coldness; to coldness succeeds neglect, and to neglect desertion. He goes away to fight the pirates in the Spanish Main, some say to join them. He is reported killed, and the report is verified, seemingly beyond the possibility of a doubt. The desolate heart of the widow turns naturally for solace toward the one whom she had loved, and who, remaining faithful to his heart's first choice, had remained unwed. He pours out upon her all the love which has been repressed during the years of her coverture. She is not only desolate but in need. He begs that she give him the right to protect and support her."

"But she is a woman of fine feeling; she respects the conventionalities. She does not wish to offend public opinion or render herself liable to adverse criticism by forming a second matrimonial alliance before the expiration of the period of mourning which convention and decorum seem to require; for she was of an old family, and proud, as our Creole ladies are justly proud. But the gentleman was pressing, her needs were also urgent,—how urgent none but herself could know. She yielded at last to her lover's importunities, and they were married privately, in a distant parish. Returning to New Orleans they resumed, to all appearances, the usual current of their lives."

"But man proposes, and God disposes. Events took such a course that three months later madame began to think that it might be well to disclose her marriage, in order to avoid harsher criticism than that which would follow a too hasty marriage—which would be, after all, but a slight thing as compared with one supposed to have been too long deferred. She had agreed with her husband that the marriage should be announced the following day. But ere it was made known the impossible happened—her former husband made his appearance in New Orleans. The report of his death, though made in good faith, had proved to be not in accordance with the facts."

"I need not ask you to picture the situation or to put yourselves in the lady's place. It was a case for heroic remedies. Innocent of wrong-doing, her good name must not be impaired. But how could it be protected? Her marriage was no marriage. Even her husband's return would not protect her; the period of his absence from the city was too well known. Upon this score, however, fortune favored her, at her husband's expense. Two days after his unexpected return, he was stabbed in a brawl in a Canal Street gambling-house, and she was left a widow in very fact and deed. The marriage ceremony was there-upon repeated in still another parish."

"But this merely relieved her of one embarrassment; there still remained the other, which the new marriage could not cure. There was but one remedy—concealment. To save the mother's good name, it was necessary temporarily to sacrifice the child. The lady retired to a distant plantation. The child was born and placed at nurse in the hands of a discreet quadroon woman, herself ignorant of its origin, and supposing it to be the child of a white father by some woman of her own class. The child's wants were amply provided for, through the medium of a discreet man of affairs, himself unaware of the real facts."

"It was the intention of the parents, after their remarriage, to adopt the child. Before this step had been taken, however, the revolution in San Domingo sent to New Orleans, among the refugees from that unhappy island, five nephews of the father of the as yet unacknowledged child,—three sons of his brother René and two of his brother Louis. To have adopted a fatherless child, to the disinheritance of his own flesh and blood, would have caused curious and unfriendly comment. Madame Beaurepas—and I need not carry the parable further, since the word is out—with her high sense of honor, her strict views of propriety, her delicate sensitiveness to public opinion, had grown morbid upon the subject of this unacknowledged son. Her nervous system broke down, and she became a chronic invalid. At any mention of her son the intensity of her emotions was such as to threaten her life. To spare her, the day of acknowledgment was allowed to remain indefinitely in the future. Upon her death my late lamented client, out of respect for her memory, chose still to keep the matter secret until his own death, which brings with it the recognition of the rights of my present respected client, M. Paul Beaurepas, who, I can say without fear of contradiction, though brought up to suppose himself a quadroon, was always amply provided for, was carefully educated, and is prepared at every point to take up the responsibilities which have been so suddenly thrust upon him. If there have arisen seeming obstacles to this, growing out of the misconception of his race, they are not such as the law, in its wise and humane provision, cannot and does not correct."

"The story has been told to my client, M. Paul Beaurepas. Indeed I asked him to be present here today, and from the next room he has heard all I have said to you."

At this, Paul Beaurepas, late Marchand, f.m.c., stepped into the room and bowed courteously to the other gentlemen, only one of whom returned his salutation, while the others glared at him with undisguised animosity. M. Renard continued:

"With the chivalrous courtesy which distinguishes the gentlemen of Louisiana, M. Paul Beaurepas has uttered not one word of blame for his father or his mother. A Creole gentleman, he is willing, in the retrospect, to have sacrificed even his life, had it been demanded, to save the honor of a lady, and especially of a lady who bore to him so close a relation. A dutiful son, he bows to his father's will. The late M. Beaurepas honored me with a measure of his confidence. It was through my agency that he provided for the support and education of his son, although I did not at the time know certainly what their relationship was. At his request I drew up this very will, leaving blank the name and description of the chief legatee, which you will observe are inserted in his own handwriting. Not until he took to his bed, ten days before he died, did he take me into his full confidence, and then only because he wished me to convey to his son certain information which he had not seen fit to embody in his will. M. Pierre Beaurepas assured me, in our last interview, that he had always kept track of his son and would have intervened to protect him in case of any threatened danger or misfortune. Indeed, he sent for him upon his deathbed, but unfortunately, because of events that evening, with the story of which you are all familiar, was not able to reach him. I should have been pleased to serve professionally whomsoever my late lamented client had chosen to be his successor. I have accepted with satisfaction and with pleasure the position of legal adviser to his heir, M. Paul Beaurepas, and shall do what I can as friend and advocate to make up to him what he has lost by virtue of the temporary obscuration of his name and social standing."

During the progress of this oration there were murmurs of incredulity, expressive shrugs and shakings of the head among the nephews. It was a pretty story, but it would not, to use a significant American expression, hold water. It was manifestly a scheme of their malicious old uncle Pierre to divert the family estate, which he in his turn had in large part inherited, from its lawful heirs, his nephews, to this quadroon by-blow, and to cover up this act of robbery by this fairy tale concocted at the expense of a lady who was dead and gone and therefore unable to defend her honor.

IX.

The Five Cousins

Paul Beaurepas, late Marchand, f.m.c., had listened to the lawyer's statements with a countenance the immobility of which cloaked a variety of emotions. When Renard declared him fitted in all respects to wear the mantle of the late Pierre Beaurepas, and hand on the traditional glory of his race, whence came the shadow that flitted momentarily across the pale olive of his cheek? When the lawyer announced that his client had no word of blame for his dead parents, was it a flash of resentment that for a moment lit up his dark eyes with a lambent flame? Or was it the glow of a chivalrous acceptance of his sponsor's statement? And when in his closing remarks Renard referred so delicately to the removal of seeming obstacles, was it regret which saddened the face of Paul Beaurepas, or tenderness which moistened his eye with a film so light that a single movement of the lids dispelled it?

Upon Marchand's appearance the cousins had instinctively drawn together at one end of the salon. M. Renard had turned to his client and stood awaiting the compliment which he expected and which came in grave tones from the lips of the heir.

"A noble deliverance, M. Renard, replete with wisdom, and legal learning and a delicate sense of honor and its obligations. With such an advocate, there can be no situation too difficult to meet, no obstacle too great to overcome."

M. Renard bowed low to the quadroon of yesterday—today the heir of Beaurepas. If there were any sarcasm in his client's voice, it was not perceptible to M. Renard, the astute lawyer, the eloquent advocate, who could read the mind of a witness like an open book; for here there was nothing at issue, nothing in doubt. As his client had said, there could be, in a matter which should naturally give rise to pleasant and indeed joyful emotions, no embarrassment which M. Renard's advice would not clear up. He had unfolded an interesting mystery in a dramatic way, had elucidated a delicate situation in a masterly manner, which had given his forensic powers full play; and he was but receiving his due meed of appreciation, which he expected as certainly and valued as much, in its own way, as the substantial fee which later on he would collect from his highly respected client.

For, from the first interview in the Calabozo, M. Renard had seen the importance of binding to himself, while yet he was alone in the field, this new-fledged great proprietor. His business as Marchand had been worth while; as Beaurepas it was vastly more important, and having conducted it for the father, it was no more than natural that he should wish to retain it for the son. Nor was he moved only by self-interest, but by a sincere desire to serve. He had always liked Paul, and liked him none the less now that he had turned out rich and powerful. With genuine pleasure and good-will, therefore, he looked forward to guiding, with tact and delicacy, his client's untried feet in the new paths where they must tread. Diplomacy would be needed to adjust the new Beaurepas to his changed environment. For M. Renard, with his knowledge of human nature, its weaknesses, its limitations, knew instinctively that although Paul Beaurepas, hitherto Marchand, had lived and moved and had his being in the same city which held within its borders the forty thousand people who made up all the grades of this curiously stratified community; though he had walked the same streets, breathed the same air, spoken the same tongue, read the same books, worn the same clothes, yet that in the kingdom of the mind, of which these other things were but the mere integument, he had lived as truly in a different world from that to which he had now received legal title of admission, as though a gulf as wide as the ocean and as deep had rolled between them.

The one particular wherein M. Renard foresaw a possible difficulty of adjustment, he had referred to, somewhat obscurely so far as the mere words went, but quite intelligibly to Paul Beaurepas, when he had spoken of the legal removal of certain seeming obstacles. M. Renard had already told Marchand, prior to the funeral, that it had been the wish and the intention of old Pierre Beaurepas, although not made a condition of the inheritance, that his heir should marry the daughter of his old friend José Morales and through her perpetuate the family name and lineage. There was, fortunately for the plan, no legal obstacle. In some of the more northern states, or in France, to which the Creole eye turned instinctively when it looked abroad, Paul's marriage to Julie Lenoir would have been valid, but the law of Louisiana made it illegal and void, and Marchand could repudiate it without legal or social reprobation and proceed to carry out his father's wishes should he so desire.

Nevertheless, M. Renard had felt rather than foreseen that he might have difficulty with his client upon this point.

Acting under instructions, he had followed, through a Paris correspondent, the student career of Paul Marchand in that city, and knew that he was a man of sentiment; that he had been an ardent Republican and had accepted and proclaimed the radical doctrine of *The Rights of Man* as applying to all men, with no reservations. Indeed M. Renard had had occasion once, shortly after his ward's return to New Orleans, to caution him because of some intemperate remark, reported to Renard, reflecting upon the morality and the economic soundness of slavery. His client, too, he had learned by inquiry, was a devoted husband and a fond father.

As a lawyer, M. Renard had found the man of sentiment a dangerous client, likely, under the stress of sudden emotion or quixotic impulse, to upset the most carefully devised plan of attack or defense—to throw, to use a modern industrial figure, a monkey-wrench into the machinery. It was far easier to handle a man who was swayed solely by self-interest, who would obey the rein and neither take the bit between his teeth nor kick over the traces. And M. Renard was not entirely certain that his client was a man of this latter class.

The group at the other end of the salon conversed in subdued but animated tones. They were, with one exception, unanimous in their condemnation of the will and their hostility to the heir.

"Our uncle was a monster!" exclaimed Raoul bitterly. "He led us to believe that we would inherit, and then cut us off without a picayune."

"Nay, cousin," said Philippe Beaurepas, "he has told each of us, many a time, that we need not hope to inherit."

"But he has told us each separately—not together; and there was no one else to inherit, so far as we knew. It was wicked, it was devilish to treat us so."

“A man,” said Philippe, “can do as he likes with his own. It is a well known maxim of the law.”

“But there is another equally trite,” retorted Raoul. “A man should so use his own as not to injure that of others. He had led us to cherish false hopes, and then has dashed them—after having waited, like a coward, until he was beyond the reach of our reproaches.”

“And he has added insult to injury,” interjected Hector, “by leaving his money to a quadroon.”

“He is a Beaurepas of the pure blood,” protested Philippe. “The proofs show it. There he stands beneath our grandfather’s portrait. He might have sat for it.”

They turned their eyes toward Paul, who stood listening gravely to the smooth flow of M. Renard’s words and apparently paying no attention to the group of cousins, no word or movement of whom, however, had escaped him.

“He has been bred a quadroon, and blood without breeding is not enough to make a gentlemen. He would disgrace the name by some Negro trait. He has been trained to subordination, to submission. How could he resent an insult? No such man can maintain the honor of the Beaurepas.”

If Honor ever blushes, as poets have asserted, she must have done it then. Only the day before, Henri Beaurepas had sold the mother of his unborn child, to whom he had promised her freedom, to pay a gambling debt!

“He has suffered more than we,” said Philippe, stoutly. “What each of you may lose, beyond the hope of wealth, I know not. I shall lose the dearest hope of my life, and I value this money not one whit except as it might have enabled me to realize this hope. Our new cousin gains the estate, but what does he not also acquire with it? The knowledge that he has been robbed, for all these years, of the sweetest things of life—a father's name, a mother's love,—of gentle breeding, of honor and renown, of the companionship of his equals—robbed of them all, too, in that happy third of life, when they are most valuable, when the fortunate youth must shine by reflected light, ere he has been able to accomplish his own career."

"A mess of sentimental nonsense," sneered Hector. "You talk like an actor in melodrama. The fellow was bred a quadroon and expected nothing better."

"He will go back," said Philippe, "for he is a man of imagination, he will go back and live over all those years in retrospect and suffer every pang which his ignorance has heretofore spared him. He has my sympathy; but for one thing, I would rather be myself than he. I shall give him my hand, and welcome him to our family."

There were murmurs of dissent, but Philippe heeded them not. He even shook off a detaining touch and walking the length of the hall, held out his hand to Paul Beaurepas, who clasped it warmly.

"Cousin," said Philippe, "your accession to your own has dashed my fondest hopes. But it was no fault of yours. I welcome you as the head of our house, and bespeak from you the friendship and interest which a cadet has a right to expect from the head of his family."

Paul Beaurepas had watched the hostile group gloomily, and somewhat wistfully. His face had lightened at Philippe's approach, without losing all its gravity.

"I thank you, cousin," he replied. "I shall not forget your loyalty and you shall not regret it. You were my well wisher I liked to think,—I would not have dared to call you friend,—when I had no claim upon your good-will."

He shot a hostile glance toward the group at the other

end of the hall, who lingered, casting furtive looks toward Philippe and muttering sarcastic comments.

"My brother and my cousins," said Philippe, "are terribly disappointed. I hope you will not judge them too harshly."

"They will feel more resigned tomorrow," said M. Renard, softly, rubbing his hands. "They will consult eminent counsel; they will see that my client's rights are unassailable, and they will think of other things which will make them reflect ere they go farther."

The group of disgruntled cousins turned to go. "Pardon me," said Philippe, "if I go with them, and try to reason with them."

When they were gone Paul Beaurepas drew from his inside pocket, a little red morocco-covered memorandum book, and turning to a list of names, struck one of them off with his lead pencil.

M. Renard prattled on. His client seemed preoccupied, but some of M. Renard's words, the lawyer felt sure, if only one here and there, would fall on fertile soil and bring forth fruit.

"You will no doubt wish to go through your father's papers, and may find something about which you will wish to consult me. Meanwhile I shall file the will for probate."

Which he did, and, as we have seen, to the surprise and wonder of all New Orleans.

X.

Julie and Her Chickens

Julie and her children were gathered in the living-room of the family home on Bourbon Street which had come to her from her father. Jacques Lenoir had been a man of culture, as evidenced by the books on the walls, most of which had been his, and of discriminating taste, as shown by the choice of the pictures and art pieces which decorated the room. There was an open piano, with sheet music on the rack, a harp, and on the table some current French novels and magazines. The interior was not so magnificent as that of the Beaurepas home on Royal Street, but the intimate touches of life and the presence of the children, made it much more comfortable, though Julie did not know it, having never been in the other house.

She was seated in a low chair, a prey to sadness. She had not seen her husband for a week and was beginning to feel anxious about him and about the future. Even the children observed her distress.

"What is the matter, maman?" babbled Bébé, coming to her mother's knee and gazing concernedly into her face.

"Yes, *petite maman*," said Celestine, "your eyes are all red. You have been crying. Your handkerchief is wet with tears. Is it about papa? Has anything happened to him? We haven't seen him for a week. What can be the matter with him?"

The little mother nerved herself for an important communication. Her ivory-tinted face, whose soft contours were generally alive with cheerfulness, took on an unusual sobriety. The fate of her children, to say nothing of her own, was trembling in the balance. Lifting the long lashes which shaded her dark eyes, she turned upon her two children,—two smaller images of herself, two doll-like creatures, clad with French daintiness in little white muslin frocks, with sashes of broad ribbon, their little heads covered with luxuriant curls which fell in natural ringlets to their waists,—a look surcharged with emotion.

"My poor children!" she exclaimed, with a tragic air.

"Yes, mama" they cried, with vague premonitions, echoing her tone and mirroring her expression.

"We have met with a great misfortune—a terrible calamity! Your papa is—"

"Our papa is dead!" they cried, bursting into loud wails.

"No, my children it is not so bad as that, for your papa, but for us it may be worse."

"What is it, mama?" demanded Celestine.

"Prepare yourselves, my angels, for terrible news. Your papa is—"

"Our papa is—"

"Your papa is—white!"

Loud was the weeping, as Julie gathered her chickens under her wings. Their papa had hated white people. Celestine had heard him declaim fiercely against their prejudice, their arrogance, their brutality and, more particularly, their slights of himself. Only a few days ago they had even heard their father swear a great French oath, that if all the white people of New Orleans had but one neck, and he could hold it in his hands, he would strike it through at a single blow, or wring it like a pullet's—b-r-r-r-r! zip!—at least, he had added a little later, after supper and a glass of wine, he would be tempted to do so. That their father should be one of these wicked white men was truly a dreadful thing.

Julie was very unhappy. She loved her husband and knew that he had loved her. But he had possessed her, and now he might leave her. She was a quadroon, and he might take to wife any one of the many beautiful unmarried white women of New Orleans,—it was inconceivable that any one of them should refuse the hand of one so handsome, so distinguished, and so rich. But his good fortune was her undoing. For her sake and her children's she wished he were still a quadroon. They would have gone away and been happy. Now they must stay in Louisiana, and she saw no way of reconciling the future with their happiness.

She consulted her confessor, Père Ambrose, but he, poor man, could give her no comfort. He was in the grip of the same forces which controlled them all, and the ghostly vicegerency of Heaven could not avail against the Louisiana code. He could only repeat the stale formula of his creed and adjure her to love God and keep his commandments, and intimate, without quite saying it, that if temptation proved too strong for her and she should sin, the Church would not refuse her absolution nor make her penance unduly severe.

XI.

The Black Drop

Paul Beaurepas, after taking possession, as we have seen, of the family mansion, went through his father's papers. The deeds, contracts, notes and securities, of which there were many, were on deposit in the vault of the Bank of New Orleans, but in his father's desk there were numerous diaries, commonplace books, and memoranda dating back for many years, throwing light upon the history and traditions of the important family of which he was called to be the head.

If he came upon any obscure point upon which he desired information, Terence, who had acted in part as his late master's secretary, and whom Paul had retained in his employment, was often able to clear it up. He had grown up with Pierre Beaurepas and knew almost as much about the family as his master—with the exception of some few things, several of which are important to this story.

Among the many letters which the late M. Beaurepas had preserved, there was a small packet, tied with a faded blue ribbon, in which Paul found a letter from Hayti, dated during the Revolution, and addressed to Pierre Beaurepas.

Paul read the letter with interest, and from it learned several things. The latter was written by Laure Beaurepas, the wife of Pierre's brother Réné, and had been penned during the horrors of the Revolution, as its uncertain handwriting and overwrought tone gave ample evidence. The writer's husband, it stated, had been killed by the insurgents, with tortures unnamable. The writer herself had been wounded, but had escaped, with her children, by the aid of her faithful servant Zabet. Dying, she confided to Zabet her three young children, together with two of her husband's brother, Louis Beaurepas, with injunctions to carry them, if possible, to their uncle in New Orleans.

"To you, my dear brother, as head of their house," she wrote, "I confide my dear children. May God deal with you as you with them, and may a mother's blessing and the love of God follow every good thing which you may do for them. I dread most leaving the little one—the others will be stronger and more able to care for themselves; but I trust in Christ and the Virgin and in you."

The letter gave Paul food for thought. He had already learned from his investigations that the parents of his cousins had been ruined in the Haytian Revolution. From this letter he gathered the manner in which his cousins had come to New Orleans. One clause only was obscure; where the writer had spoken of the little one, she had used the feminine form, "*la petite.*" His five cousins were all males. Was this a grammatical error, due to the writer's stress of emotion? Or, if not, who was the girl, and what had become of her, and whence had come the fifth male cousin? It was a subject too delicate to question Terence upon directly, so he merely asked the butler if the late M. Beaurepas had ever had a niece, to which question Terence returned a negative answer.

The next day he sent a servant for old Zabet. She came smiling and curtseying, expecting a reward. Had not her prophecy been fulfilled? Was not the former quadroon now white, and rich and powerful, and in the way to obtain all the rest that she had promised him? Surely he would be liberal, nay, more than liberal, even generous.

"Good day, Zabet."

"Good day, Master Paul. My dream came true!"

"It was no dream, Zabet. Your prophecy came true in part, and you shall be rewarded—that is, when you shall have answered me three questions."

"Three hundred, master, if old Zabet could know so many things."

He motioned her to a seat. She sat down upon the edge of it, and watched him shrewdly through narrowed eyes. His aspect was serious, not to say severe, and she felt vague forebodings.

"When you left Hayti with the children of my uncles, there were five. How many did you bring to New Orleans."

"Five, master; three of Miché Réné and two of your Uncle Louis. Have you not five cousins?"

"What became of the little one, the girl?"

"The girl, Master Paul?" she stammered. "There was no girl. I brought only boys. Every one knows it, they have grown up in the house. They are known to all New Orleans."

"Yes, Zabet, but when you left Hayti, there was a girl!"

"No, master, five boys! I swear it! five boys, Raoul, Hector, Adolphe, Henri and Philippe, five nephews of your father, Pierre Beaurepas! I swear it before God and the Virgin! May I be struck dead in my tracks if it be not so!"

Paul Beaurepas was not satisfied. Zabet protested too much; she was as much too vehement as too palpably afraid.

He rose, went to the door and locked it. Zabet followed his movements with a fearful curiosity. He took from a closet a rawhide whip, such as overseers used to chastise slaves, and from a drawer a pistol, which he loaded and primed deliberately, and from a hook where it was suspended, his sword, and laid them side by side upon the table.

Zabet followed his movements with the fascination of terror. What did he mean to do? Old Pierre Beaurepas had been a hard man, but with a vein of cynical humor and with lapses of humanity. This new Beaurepas's face was set like a stone mask. Zabet's flesh began to creep with apprehension, which was only partially allayed when Beaurepas drew from another drawer a rouleau of gold pieces, which he placed beside the weapons.

"Zabet," he said, "you are my slave."

"But, master," she stammered, "I am free—my mistress gave me my freedom."

"You are my slave, Zabet. You were never legally freed. You are mine, by inheritance from my father."

"He never claimed me—I have been free for thirty years."

"Then if you are not mine, you belong to my cousins."

"God forbid!" muttered Zabet, crossing herself.

"You see upon the table an inkstand, in which is a pen, with one stroke of which I can transfer you to a slave dealer. You are old, but still capable of much hard work."

"Mother of God, save me!" whispered Zabet.

"There is here a whip. If with it I should beat you to death, no one would have a word to say!"

"You would not do it, master," she moaned. "There were five boys—I swear it!"

"With one stroke of this pen, I could write an order to Valdez, at the calaboose, to loosen your tongue."

Zabet trembled. Never in her life had she been whipped, but she knew what such an order meant, and knew, furthermore, that none would gainsay it. So Zabet trembled and the blood in her veins stood still.

Beaurepas went on, coldly and incisively:

"A touch of this pistol, a thrust of this sword, and you would go to meet your God, Zabet, with all your sins upon your soul."

Zabet had no wish to die. She had not confessed for a month and there had always been reservations, held for her last confession. Nor did she wish to give up life; too old to sin, she could still enjoy the savor and cherish the memory of past offenses.

"Master," she muttered shakily, her eyes evading his, "there were five boys."

Paul Beaurepas strode over to the trembling hag and seized her by the arm.

"Down on your knees, huzzy!" he thundered, "Down on your knees and tell me the truth, or take your choice—the slave gang, the whip, the pistol, or the sword."

With one hand he forced her to her knees, and with the other reached toward the table.

"There were four boys, and a girl, master, when I left the island."

"Ah!"

Paul Beaurepas released his hold on Zabet's arm and left her groveling on the floor.

"Go on!" he said, "go on!"

"The little girl died,—there were too many, the ship was small and crowded, the sea was high, the sun was hot, the water was stagnant, there was no milk—the little girl died."

"Who was the fifth boy?"

"Your uncle Réné's child, master, and my daughter's! His child as much as any! I brought the child with me, and when the little girl died, I brought the boy instead to Pierre Beaurepas—who was also *his* uncle!"

A look flashed over Beaurepas's face, a look which boded ill for some one though not for Zabet, for the tone in which he now addressed her was kind. Having won his point he could afford to be magnanimous.

"Get up, old woman," he said, lifting her to her feet. "You have told the truth. One question more, and one more truthful answer, and the roll of gold is yours. Which of my cousins was the fifth child?"

Zabet's face fell. "Master," she pleaded, "you'll not be hard on him? You know what it is not to be white?"

"Oh, no, Zabet. I shall do to him no more than he deserves. His name?"

She whispered a name in his ear. The sinister look, which had disfigured his countenance and might very well have marked the joy of anticipated revenge, gave place, after Zabet had spoken, to an expression very like disappointment.

XII.

The Honor of the Family

Despite his outward calm, Paul Beaurepas, during the weeks which had passed since the discovery of his birth, had gone through a fiery furnace of emotion. No one but a man of spirit finding himself in that condition could quite have known what it was to belong to an inferior caste in a city like New Orleans. Even the Negroes retained a measure of natural dignity and self-respect, which slavery had not been able to eradicate entirely and which yearned dumbly for recognition, and the proud blood of French gentlemen, even when mingled with that of slaves, some times clamored passionately for its birthright.

He had lost so much! He had enjoyed much, it is true, in comparison with others less fortunate; but we too often measure our happiness by what we lack and not by what we have. Paul Marchand, free man of color, had possessed a certain degree of wealth and education. He had therefore resented all the more fiercely the deprivation of civil rights and social opportunities. His pride had in a measure sustained him; but one man's pride was a weak barrier against a whole world's scorn, and to Paul Marchand and all who dwelt within its borders, the Crescent City was the world, and the white people within it the people thereof. The others were permitted to live, like the slaves, because they were useful to the whites, or, as the free people of color, by sufferance. Slave or free, they had no rights which white men might not override. That there was left to those who were free some measure of comfort and pleasure; that not all white men were tyrannical and unjust; that the quadroons were envied by the blacks far more than they were despised by the whites, consoled some of them, but had never satisfied Paul Marchand. Whether it were blood or temperament, he had cared very little what the Negroes might think of him,—he had pitied them with a profound pity, but had never counted himself as one of them. Thus, between two castes, he had grown into a proud isolation, which had developed into a bitterness that the revelation of his birth could not all at once assuage, but rather, as Philippe suggested at the reading of the will, even tended to accentuate.

As had been predicted by M. Renard, the cousins took counsel among themselves and with lawyers, and decided that discretion was the better part of valor. In the consultation it came out that each of them was heavily indebted to the estate. The purpose of old Pierre in bringing this about was so obvious that no one of them imagined for a moment that Paul did not have the notes of hand they had given their uncle. Having been advised that a contest of the will would provide futile, that there was no possible ground for claiming that undue influence had procured its making, and that both church and state were interested in maintaining its validity, their interests obviously required that they placate the heir, in order that the tradition of the house in reference to the younger members should not be broken. It was decided to give a family dinner at the home of Henri, at which their new cousin should be the guest of honor. It was in effect the ancient service of fealty. They would acclaim their cousin as the head of the house, break with him the bread of hospitality, and drink to his happiness in the wine of fellowship. No formal invitation was issued, but Philippe undertook the task of inviting Paul to honor the occasion with his presence. Paul signified his assent with the grave dignity which had marked his manner since his sudden accession to wealth and social position.

It was a men's party. Henri chanced to be in funds, and the table was elegantly appointed. The dinner, sent in from a hotel, was prepared by a *cordon bleu*, and served by well trained waiters. The conversation was general, and upon topics of current interest, seeming to avoid by mutual consent the matter of the inheritance and the circumstances attending it. The formal part of the entertainment was reserved until after the coffee had been served. At this point Henri Beaurepas, who had been chosen as spokesman, having filled his glass, rose to his feet and cleared his throat. Instantly silence reigned and every eye was turned upon him.

"Gentlemen and cousins," he began in conventional phrase, "we are gathered together here upon this auspicious occasion to unite in an act which we owe to the honor of our house and to the memory of our distinguished relative and benefactor. By a strange fate, for which no one of us is responsible, our cousin Paul Beaurepas, having been for many years deprived of his birth-right as the son and heir presumptive of our uncle Pierre, has come into his own. If any of us had been led, through ignorance of the real facts, to anticipate a different disposition of our uncle's estate, it too was equally with no fault of ours. The Beaurepas family has long been one of the glories of Louisiana. It took its root with the birth of the colony and we all hope that it may survive and maintain its prestige so long as this fair city shall stand. Its fate, for the next generation, rests in the hands of our relative, M. Paul Beaurepas, our honored guest upon this occasion. That he may prove more than equal to this responsibility is our earnest wish, our fond hope, and our confident expectation."

"As cadets of this distinguished family, it will be our duty as well as our pleasure to hold up the hands of our fortunate relative in all things that may tend to maintain the honor and dignity of our name. As younger members of the family we desire to feel ourselves free to seek at the hands of the head of our house that sympathy and support which his commanding position will so well enable him to extend. We have therefore gathered here tonight to cement with friendship the ties of blood which already unite us to him. Gentlemen and cousins, I propose the health of our cousin, Paul Beaurepas!"

The toast was drunk with much show of enthusiasm, and when the glasses rested again upon the table all eyes were turned toward Paul. He rose from his seat and spoke with the gravity which had characterized him for the past week.

"Gentlemen and cousins," he said, "I thank you for this expression of loyalty toward one whom fate has so suddenly and unexpectedly thrust into your lives and the life of your family—*our* family. Such a tender of fealty demands an adequate response. Ordinarily there could be but one reply to such an offer. But the very unusual circumstances of my upbringing, for which I find no fault with any one, have created upon my part a situation equally unusual, and impel me to make a somewhat different course from what might be expected. No one could know so well as you the Beaurepas crest, a mailed arm erect, the hand holding a sword, with the motto *"Coup pour Coup"*—"Blow for Blow," nor could any one so well as you appreciate the principle which has always governed the Beaurepas in affairs of honor. That principle is, as our motto implies and as you well know, that an insult can only be wiped out with blood. Other men, with milk in their veins, might accept an apology for a blow—words for deeds—but no Beaurepas has ever yet accepted an apology without having first crossed swords with his insulter. I take it that I can do no less than maintain the honor of my house—*our* house—nor can I imagine for one moment a scion of that stock acting upon any other rule. Before, therefore, responding to the toast which you have drunk to me, I deem it my duty to search the history of my past and see if there is between myself and any gentleman here present, any matter which involves the honor of the family, or of myself as its representative. If there be, then I know that no one of you would ask or expect of me such a compact of friendship until this cause of offense has first been removed."

The Beaurepas cousins were looking at one another with wonder in their eyes. What bee had this regenerated quadroon in his bonnet? What card had this parvenu Beaurepas up his sleeve? What did it all mean?

Vague memories stirred within them. They were not long kept in suspense. Paul Beaurepas drew from his breast pocket a small morocco-covered memorandum book which he opened and held before him under the light of the wax candles which shimmered in the chandelier above the table.

"I have here," he said, "a little memorandum, made by me at various times during the past year, by reference to which I find that on the first of October last, at the instance of M. Henry Beaurepas, a lease which I had taken of a box in the second tier of the Opera House was canceled; that on the second of January, on the complaint of M. Adolphe Beaurepas, I was refused service in a restaurant on Canal Street; that on April the tenth I was slapped in the face by M. Raoul Beaurepas on the *vieux carré* in front of the cathedral; that on the fifteenth, in a dispute with M. Hector Beaurepas, in the cotton exchange, he called me to my face a Negro, and a pig, and said that he would slit my ears, but that it would defile his sword; again at the instance of M. Henri Beaurepas, I was ignominiously expelled from a ball at the Salle Condé, on which occasion, in defending myself from unwarranted assault, I happened to strike M. Henri, and, also at his instance, I presume, I was incarcerated in the Calabozo, where I spent several unhappy hours. Some of these were small matters, perhaps, or might at the time have seemed to be, but can I, as a Beaurepas, enter into a compact of friendship with gentlemen, however closely related, who having thus offended me have not satisfied, in the traditional way, the honor of the Beaurepas?"

There was never a more astonished company. This cousin of theirs, while yet to all intents and purposes a quadroon, had treasured every slight, had marked it down with day and date; and to what end? He could have had at that time no inkling of his birth or prospects. For what reason, except for a hypothetical revenge which he could have had no probable means of realizing, could he have pursued such a course? To their superstitious minds it almost appeared as though some supernatural influence had taken this cousin of theirs under its protection and led him to do instinctively this curious and dangerous thing. It was a proof, too, if any were needed, of his purity of race. No quadroon could have taken such a course, it was foreign to the quadroon nature.

Henri Beaurepas was the first to find speech.

"Cousin," said he, conciliatingly, "we perceive with pride that our uncle's mantle has fallen upon worthy shoulders.

You have justly stated the unwritten law of our family. But to even so well established a rule there may be exceptions. By the law, as I have been advised, the intention is an essential element of the offense. If perchance in passing through a crowded street I accidentally brush against a gentleman and cause him to lose his footing and fall, judged by my lack of intent I have committed no offense for which an apology would not be ample satisfaction. If, on the contrary, I have of set purpose and with hostile intent but laid the weight of my little finger upon a man's person, I have committed upon him an assault which the law would punish by fine and imprisonment, and which by the code of honor could only be wiped out by an abject apology or by blood, and, by the Beaurepas code, by blood alone."

"By blood alone," echoed Paul, softly.

"But, cousin," continued Henri, "applying this rule, there was in your case no intent to offend. To us Paul Beaurepas did not exist; and we could not insult one who had not come into being. The acts of which you complain were directed against a certain *soi-disant* quadroon, who, in his turn, no longer exists. A white man could not insult a man of color, and therefore there was no insult."

"Pardon me, cousin, Paul Beaurepas—I who speak to you—was not born yesterday, but twenty-five years ago. It was this cheek," he said, laying his hand against it, "it was this same cheek that tingled with the blow. It was these ears which burned with the offensive epithet, and which would have listened to the music of the opera. It was these feet which carried me into the ballroom; it was these bones, gentlemen, which lay upon the cold stones of the calaboose—they are sore yet from the contact; it was these lungs that drank in the vile air of the prison. And it is this cheek, these ears, it is all these that clamor for satisfaction. Gentlemen, I echo your wish that there shall be none but pleasant relations between us. But my conscience will not permit me to accept your friendship until I shall have proved my title to the honor of a Beaurepas."

Philippe was next to speak.

"Our cousin Paul," he said, "is right. He could not do otherwise. He has not called my name. But if I have at any time offended him, though unwittingly, I am ready to accord him the satisfaction of a gentleman."

"Our cousin," added Adolphe, suavely, "does not, I am sure, thirst for our blood. To cross swords with us will be enough to satisfy his honor—the honor of the family."

"It is his right," said Hector, "and we acknowledge it. It is brave of our cousin thus to stand upon his right. For we, because of our upbringing, are skilful with the sword, while he, because of his, can have no familiarity with it. Nevertheless, he would defend his honor at any risk. I think I speak for all of us when I say that this meeting or these meetings will be but a mere formality, for no one of us would take advantage of our cousin's want of knowledge of the gentleman's weapon."

"Certainly," they all assented. "It will be but a mere formality."

If Paul Beaurepas, late Marchand, felt any inclination to smile as he listened, it was indicated by nothing more than an almost imperceptible parting of the lips.

"Gentlemen and cousins," he said, "I thank you. That you could give no other answer I well knew, and that I could take no other course was equally apparent. As the challenged, it is your privilege to name the time and place of meeting."

"Since there are four of us and but one of you," said Raoul, "we waive the privilege. Fix your time and place and we will be in attendance."

"The Oaks, with swords, at six o'clock, day after tomorrow morning," said Paul promptly. "Tomorrow is the Sabbath and we will wait until Monday."

"Our new cousin," said Hector to Henri, when Paul had gone away, "seems to take the family honor *au grand serieux.*"

"It is a new toy, and he likes to play with it," returned Henri. "Then, too, it is the zeal of the proselyte,—he wishes to do something spectacular and un-African to make people forget the Negro that he was."

"He is either very stupid, or very subtle," replied Hector. "We shall have to watch our step."

"It is a matter," said Henri, "for deep thought. Our cousin, too, had best be careful."

XIII.

A Tip from Perigord

Adolphe Beaurepas, sauntering idly along Royal Street on Sunday afternoon, on his way to the *Café des Exilés,* where he had an appointment with a San Domingan gentleman, to arrange the details of a cock fight, met Guillaume Perigord, the fencing-master.

"*Bon jour,* M. Beaurepas," exclaimed Perigord, with the military salute which he affected.

"*Bon jour,* Perigord," returned Adolphe, "how do you carry yourself?"

"Very well, thank you. And you, monsieur?"

"Passably. What could you expect, after an earthquake—a revolution. The cursed will of my uncle—"

"Ah, yes," returned the other with seeming sympathy. "It was astonishing, almost incredible. But truth is stranger than fiction. And the duel—it is curious, what I have heard, if it be correct?"

"What have you heard, Perigord?"

"*Pardieu,* that M. Paul Beaurepas is to meet each of his five cousins tomorrow morning, consecutively, in satisfaction of certain insults which he received as Paul Marchand, free man of color."

"It is true, Perigord, but—"

"I wonder he is not afraid! The Beaurepas are good swordsmen. Five to one are large odds."

"Certainly, Perigord, but it will be a mere formality. It is a tradition of our house that for an insult one must fight. Our cousin must, for the honor of the family, cross swords with us. It will be a mere formality—our cousin's upbringing has not been such as to give him skill with the gentleman's weapon."

"Ah, that is well. Your cousin has great confidence in your magnanimity. He has so much at stake! If the duel were *à l'outrance* who knows what might happen? A stroke, a thrust, and the estate would descend a second time, all in a week—but, then that would do you no good; your cousin is married and has children who would inherit."

"Not so, Perigord! As a man of color, he was married; as a white man, he is not. His wife is his mistress, his children bastards. Were the meeting a real one, or should there be an accident, the estate would go to the legal heirs, his cousins."

Perigord smiled grimly. The Beaurepas cousins were known by reputation to all New Orleans, and there had been few to sympathize with their chagrin.

Adolphe started to resume his walk.

"But, M. Beaurepas," suggested the fencing-master, with a seriousness of tone which masked a sly smile, "it is well, too, for M. Paul's cousins, that this meeting is a mere formality."

"And why so, Perigord?"

"For a very good reason. I will tell you a secret—M. Paul Beaurepas is the best swordsman in New Orleans."

Adolphe Beaurepas's mouth opened wide with surprise, and stood open until, with an effort, he found speech.

"But it is impossible! He has been brought up colored, and colored men do not bear arms!"

"You forget that he was educated in Paris. I knew him there; he was a pupil of Jaures, my own master. Even M. Henri Beaurepas cannot touch him. I have seen him put five men *hors de combat* in ten minutes. He was at my *atelier* last night, practicing with me certain difficult passes."

Adolphe endeavored to conceal his surprise, as, repeating the remark that the meeting was a mere formality, he left Perigord and went on down the street. This news of Perigord's was disturbing, to say the least. That Paul Marchand-Beaurepas was a skilful swordsman might well be—in a Paris *salle d'armes* a quadroon might fence with a nobleman. But why should he be practicing passes with a fencing-master? Did he suspect treachery, and mean to be on his guard against it? Or did he secretly cherish some deep scheme of revenge, and mean to wipe out the whole family? Adolphe himself was a poor hand with the saber. The possibility of accident had been foreseen, by the challenged cousins, but Adolphe, with the rest, had rather expected that such an accident might take place in the encounter with Henri. It had indeed been arranged that Adolphe should first cross swords with the challenger, then Raoul, then Hector, and then, when the formal character of the meeting had been completely established, an accident might happen which would change the succession. They had not actually planned such a thing, but the possibility of it had been in the minds of them all.

But suppose that Paul Beaurepas were vindictive? He, Adolphe, would be at his mercy; he would be first to meet him. If *he* should be the victim of an accident—the prospect was not so pleasing! If he were not present, he would run no risk. Suppose the worst—or rather, suppose that Paul Beaurepas should kill one of the cousins, or two, and then, wearied by his efforts, should fall by Henri's sword? Adolphe could only profit by such an event. In no way could he suffer by remaining away from the meeting, and in no way could he profit by warning his cousins. If one or more of them were killed, there would be fewer for the head of the house to favor. If the head of the house succumbed, he, Adolphe, would share the estate with the others without running any risk; in the very improbable event of the whole party being wiped out, in a miniature battle of Roncesvalles, he, Adolphe, would be the sole heir to the Beaurepas millions!

But these reflections, however pleasing, were but dreams. He turned back to where the fencing master was standing looking after him quizzically.

"As I have said, Perigord, it will be a mere formality. Please say nothing to the others, if you meet them, about my cousin's skill. There's no need to disturb their equanimity. The meeting will be a mere formality, to satisfy an imaginary point of honor."

XIV.

The Duel

The meeting which Paul Beaurepas had demanded of his cousins took place at "The Oaks," the fashionable Creole dueling ground, a cleared vacant space several squares north of the cathedral, marked by three large water-oaks. While the place and time of the meeting had not been advertised, enough about it had leaked out to draw a small knot of curious spectators, who kept themselves in the background, however, behind the screening shrubbery which surrounded the dueling ground.

The gentlemen met and exchanged formal greetings. There had come of Paul's five cousins only four. Philippe was present, though not among those challenged.

"Our cousin Adolphe," suggested Paul, "will doubtless appear later. Shall we wait or proceed?"

"Let us go on," said Hector. "He will appear."

"I will answer for him, cousin," said Philippe.

At that moment a colored messenger came up and handed Paul a note.

"Pardon me, gentlemen," he said, as he broke the seal and glanced at the writing, which he thereupon stuck in his belt. The gentlemen had removed their coats and waistcoats and were in their shirt-sleeves.

The contestants had agreed to fight without seconds. There being no mortal offense, it had been agreed that the character of the meeting would permit them to dispense with some of the usual formalities. Henri Beaurepas, representing the challenged, had selected sabers as the weapon, to which Paul had assented. Nothing had been stipulated as to the length of the swords, and if Henri Beaurepas had provided himself with one unusually long, Paul Beaurepas gave no sign of having observed it.

"Are you ready?"

Raoul Beaurepas advanced and drew his weapon.

"On guard!"

After a few preliminary passes their sabers clashed. Pass followed pass, thrust was countered with thrust. Raoul was a good though not a brilliant fencer. Paul Beaurepas, handling his weapon in what seemed to the casual observer an awkward manner, kept to the defense for several minutes, but finally, as their swords clashed in midair, Paul's weapon seemed to slip downward and the point made a slight wound in Raoul's left cheek.

It had been agreed that the drawing of blood on either side should end that particular encounter.

Paul Beaurepas was profuse in his apologies.

"My cousin Raoul, and you, gentlemen, will pardon my awkwardness. It is due, of course, to my ignorance and lack of skill, the result of my upbringing. I could have deferred this meeting, of course, until I had taken a few more lessons and could have met you on more nearly equal terms. But you are doubtless as anxious as I to get these little matters out of the way, and to that end will consent to undergo any temporary inconvenience attending the process."

"It is nothing," said Raoul. "Were this a real encounter, I should be ready to go on."

"No," returned Paul, "I am satisfied. By a rare coincidence my sword has scratched you in the precise spot where you so impulsively struck me in the *vieux carré*. Who is next?"

Hector Beaurepas stepped forward.

"On guard!"

This Beaurepas, the most quarrelsome of the family, was a better swordsman than Raoul. Moreover he was beginning to suspect that Paul Beaurepas was more skilled than he would have them believe, and was therefore strictly on guard from the moment their swords clashed. He made stroke after stroke, tierce, carte, thrust and counterthrust, each of which was parried by Paul with seeming awkwardness but with unvarying success. At length Paul assumed the offensive, Hector defended himself cleverly, but finally in a sudden and seemingly awkward lunge which Hector sought unsuccessfully to parry, the edge of Paul's sword slit the right ear of his adversary downward from the top for about half an inch.

"*Pardieu*, cousin!" exclaimed Hector angrily,—he was boiling with rage and could hardly contain himself,—"but you are most damnably awkward. You might have put out my eye. Deliver me from amateur fencers!"

"I crave your pardon, cousin. It is but a little thing—no more than you said, at the cotton market, that you would have liked to do to me had you not feared to defile your sword. It will leave only a slight scar, and I have not soiled my sword. I am entirely satisfied. I trust you bear no malice?"

Hector grumbled something which might have been an assent and stepped to the rear.

"And now my cousin Henri? I shall have to watch myself with you, cousin, or I shall come off second best. On guard!"

Henri Beaurepas had no longer any illusions about the swordsmanship of his cousin Paul. That he was a good fencer, a better one than either of the men he had met, was perfectly plain. His pretense of awkwardness did not deceive Henri, nor was he any longer in doubt as to his cousin's purpose. This contest was no mere formality. It was being fought by Paul Beaurepas with a definite though so far obviously not a deadly intention, and Henri was determined to secure, if possible, the advantage. His purpose was less pacific. Aside from any question of the estate, his reputation as a swordsman was at stake. He was quite willing to kill his cousin if he could.

He set out to force the fighting, but the first few passes convinced him that he might as well dismiss his sinister purpose, and that he would do well himself to escape maiming. He tried every form of attack—the press, the lunge, the thrust, the riposte,—but all were met and foiled. He feinted, but never caught Paul off his guard. His long sword could never quite reach his adversary. He tried several tricks which he had learned from Perigord, but Paul seemed to sense them at the first movement and met or parried them all.

As the fighting grew fast and furious, the spectators pressed forward from behind the shrubbery, until the contestants were surrounded by a ring of eager-faced young men who added by their cries and applause to the excitement of the occasion. Finally in making a rather low thrust which

Henri tried unsuccessfully to parry, the point of Paul's weapon found lodgment in the upper part of his adversary's thigh.

Henri dropped his sword and clapped his hand to his wound.

"It is too bad," said Paul, ruefully. "I am very sorry. You will need a surgeon."

At this moment a man with an instrument case made his way to the fore.

"I took the liberty," said Paul, "of asking Dr. Duchesne to be in attendance, in case I might require his services for myself, or lest awkwardness, in spite of the best intentions, might have some such untoward result as indeed it has had. But it is partly your own fault, cousin Henri. You are the better fencer and you pressed me too hard. Your sword, too, is much longer—I shudder to think of what might have happened had *you* proved awkward. I trust the wound is not serious, doctor?"

"No," replied the surgeon, "but he will not be able to dance for a month or six weeks."

" 'Tis a great pity," returned Paul, "for no one loves so well as he to dance. The Salle de Condé balls will miss him. But, gentlemen, I think this terminates our meeting."

"Not so," said Philippe, who had been an eager spectator. "My brother Adolphe has not arrived."

"He has sent a note," replied Paul with an imperceptible smile, as he drew from his belt the paper which the boy had brought him. "He writes that, owing to a touch of inflammatory rheumatism in his sword arm, he regrets most profoundly that he must ask me to defer our meeting until some later date.

"But the honor of the family," said Philippe, "is not satisfied. Since Adolphe is not here, I will meet you in his stead. You have been offended, you are entitled to satisfaction, and I will not permit my brother to defeat you of it."

"But I've no quarrel with you, cousin," returned Paul. "Your honor is not impugned by his absence."

"But that of the family is. You are the head of the family, but not the sole custodian of its honor and traditions. We also bear the name. I shall assume my brother's obligation and cross swords with you in his stead."

"As you will," replied Paul, indifferently.

They placed themselves on guard. After a few passes, by a quick side stroke, Paul sent Philippe's weapon flying about ten feet behind him. Philippe recovered it and would have gone on.

"No, no, cousin," said Paul, "it is enough, and you have saved your point. You have done a gallant and a chivalrous thing. I admire your spirit, but have not the heart to fight you. I do not want your blood nor do I wish you to draw mine. I have upheld the family tradition and wiped out my insults in blood,—a very little of it was enough—and I have nothing but the kindest and most kinsmanly feeling for you all."

These were fair words, if not, in view of what had just happened, entirely convincing. A carriage had been brought for Henri, and he was driven away for further attention. The other gentlemen, followed by a crowd of spectators who had gathered during the altercation, made their way back to the city.

The duel, or rather the wholesale meeting between Paul and his cousins, created only a less sensation than had the will of old Pierre, and the community was kept as busy guessing about it as certain of the Beaurepas were in explaining. Paul was the most talked of man in New Orleans. That a man, reared as he had been, should stand up face to face against four gentlemen born and bred, and place them all *hors de combat,* was a wonderful thing, and not entirely explained by the theory that the cousins, out of deference to their cousin Paul's lack of swordsmanship, had permitted him to slit the ear of one, gash the cheek of another, and to well-nigh hamstring a third, reputedly the best fencer in New Orleans, not to mention disarming the other.

Nor was the explanation that the meeting was a mere formality at all convincing. That a man should slice several others up more or less completely, and seemingly at his own sweet will, as a mere formality, was even less likely than that four fire-eating Beaurepas should willingly submit to such treatment, especially with the odds so much in their favor. Adolphe Beaurepas's absence from the meeting was the subject of caustic comment, his rheumatism was openly scoffed at, and his reputation suffered still further from some reference by Perigord at his *atelier* to their conversation before the duel.

There was less said to Paul Beaurepas than to any one else concerning the matter. His manner did not invite confidence or familiarity. Those who had scorned him as a man of color felt some natural delicacy about forcing themselves upon him as a white man. It was felt that it would be better to leave these matters to time and circumstance. They would of course adjust themselves.

XV.

Don José Pays His Respects

Don José Morales called upon the heir of Beaurepas soon after his succession.

"Monsieur," he said, "I wish to pay my respects to the son of my old friend. I wish it had been my privilege years ago. I have heard your father criticized for leaving you so long in ignorance of your birth. But he was my friend; do not think too harshly of him."

"Never fear, Señor Morales, I have not uttered one word of reproach against him. Did he not, by the stroke of his pen, lift me from the painful condition of a quadroon—a Negro—to the exalted position of a member of the best white family in Louisiana, excepting, of course, your own? He might never have told me. I might have remained always a quadroon and worn out my heart with useless repining."

"You are a good son, and will make a good father."

"I am a father already."

"Ah, yes," replied the old Spaniard with a fine smile, "we know—young blood flows swiftly in our climate. But you must have sons to inherit the name and the estate of Beaurepas; it is a duty you owe to your family and to society."

Paul Beaurepas smiled to himself somewhat grimly. So far at least, the debit side of his social account was not of impressive magnitude.

"You will make a good father, if you have the right mother for your children. Come out to Trois Pigeons and see us. Your father came every month. My daughter will be glad to know you. Your father loved her."

"Thank you, Don José, I shall come."

Old Morales still lingered.

"By the way, Paul,—I shall call you Paul, I called your father Pierre—there was a matter between your father and me."

"A matter?" he returned.

"Yes, a mortgage on my plantation. It has been running many years, and I fear the interest is somewhat in default. May I hope that you will be an lenient as your father?"

"Do not disturb yourself for the present, Señor Morales. I have not yet looked thoroughly into the affairs of the estate. Until I am better informed do not disturb yourself."

This was not strictly true, but he had not cared to anticipate what he foresaw Don José had come to say. He had learned of course, of the mortgage on Trois Pigeons, and was entirely familiar with the state of the account, but for certain reasons did not wish to commit himself at this time.

Old Morales went away, relieved but not entirely satisfied. He had hoped that Philippe would be the heir of Beaurepas, or if not Philippe, one of the other nephews, with a provision conditioning the inheritance upon marriage with Joséphine, or at least, a clause forgiving the debt. But none of these things had happened. Pierre Beaurepas, with his malicious humor, must have chuckled to himself upon his deathbed at the prospect of the complications to which the will and the astounding revelations attending it would give rise.

"He was my friend, but if I am broken," mused old Morales, as he rode away, "if I have to give up Trois Pigeons, I shall say he was a damned scoundrel. He led me to think that I should never have to pay the debt, and then he dies and leaves it to a stranger, his son,—he says—he is the image of him, and he has no sign of Negro blood—but at heart an alien to our race and caste. I am between the devil and the deep sea. This Beaurepas is smooth-spoken; his words are very dutiful, but not once in our interview did he refer to old Pierre as his father. I am not sure of him, unless he shall come to see Joséphine. She is beautiful, and few men could resist her. I have promised her to Pierre for his heir. It is a pity about the other woman, but—what of it? She is a quadroon and that ends it. She can be provided for; it is done every day."

He rode home, dismounted, threw his bridle to a slave, and sought his daughter. He found her pale and hollow-eyed, with traces of tears upon her cheeks.

"Joséphine," he said, "all is not yet lost, but whether or not we shall leave Trois Pigeons and face ruin depends upon you."

"Oh, father, I can do nothing. Philippe was disinherited."

"It is not a question of Philippe, my child. Philippe, as you say, is disinherited. As he had understood all along, he was to marry you if he were the heir. But Pierre Beaurepas has tricked us all; Philippe is not the heir and therefore you are not for him."

"But I love him, father."

"Silence, Joséphine! No well-bred maiden should love

where she cannot marry. There is another; the heir himself has promised to come and see you."

"Father!" exclaimed Joséphine with indignation, "a quadroon to visit me—to visit us!"

"*Peste*, Joséphine! the man is no quadroon, but as handsome a white man as we know."

"But he has a wife."

"A quadroon wife, my dear, whom neither the law nor the church recognizes."

"But they have children!"

"Quadroon children, my daughter, bastards. Their mother's status fixes theirs."

"I could never bear the sight of him," declared Joséphine. "He has been brought up as a Negro. He must feel as a Negro, think as a Negro; I could never be sure of him. Besides, father, I love Philippe!"

"I forbid you to love Philippe," said Morales, sternly, "and order you to make yourself agreeable to the man whose word can make us paupers. I promised you to old Pierre's heir, and by God! I shall keep my word!"

Joséphine said nothing, but cried her eyes out, and waited for Philippe. But Philippe had not come; indeed, her father had sought him out, after the will was published, had frankly stated the hopelessness of his passion, and had forbidden him the house.

So Joséphine cried her eyes out, but Philippe did not come. She sent a letter to him by a slave, and received a reply by the same means. The messenger dared not risk his hide by taking another—he stood in mortal terror of Mendoza's lash. So Joséphine cried her eyes out, and stopped between her tears only long enough to eat and sleep; for rarely does youth lose its appetite for either. And she swore that if her father married her to this white-quadroon, or this quadroon-white, she would give him cause to regret his choice—she loved Philippe and would never love any one else!

XVI.

At Trois Pigeons

One morning, glancing at the daily newspaper, Paul gave a mighty start. An item on the first page announced the escape, from the city prison, of two prisoners—a Negro and a mulatto,—who had been arrested two weeks before as runaways, on the plantation of Trois Pigeons, and sentenced to be sold as vagrants. They answered to the names of Jean Lebeau, or *Grande-Tête*, and Pedro Valdez, or *le Borgne*—the one-eyed. A description of their persons followed, with the statement that they had last been seen making their way westward and that a posse had been sent in pursuit of them.

Paul's memory ran swiftly back to the colloquy he had overheard in the Calabozo, between the inmates of the cell adjoining his own, and a swift vision rose before him, of a broken levee and a wide plantation flooded; of a house in flames, and of a young woman at the mercy of two wretches brutalized by slavery, maddened by unjust imprisonment, burning with the fire of revenge. Paul Beaurepas had a substantial interest in Trois Pigeons plantation; in fact it belonged to him whenever he chose to claim possession, and any damage to it was an injury to himself. But not for one moment did this view of the matter occur to him. The danger to Joséphine dwarfed every other thought.

He recalled the plot he had overheard in the prison. He had not the slightest doubt that the escaped prisoners would make their way toward Trois Pigeons. They were desperate men;—like Ishmael, every man's hand was against them, and theirs against every man. Sure to die, sooner or later, by violence, they would live only to gratify strong passions—lust and drink and gaming and revenge. By sacking Trois Pigeons they might sate them all. Even now, thought Paul, they might be killing the master and the overseer, firing the house, or cutting the levee.

He hastily summoned old Terence and ordered his best horse saddled and brought around. Buckling on a sword and thrusting a pistol in his belt, he mounted and rode away toward Trois Pigeons.

It had been raining for several days. The road was muddy and the riding hard, and Paul's good horse, pressed to his utmost, was tired ere he reached the outskirts of the plantation. As he neared the river and looked across the cotton fields he saw men running toward the river, with spades and shovels in their hands. The first step had been taken. The miscreants had cut the levee, and quick work would be necessary to save the bottoms from inundation. The next step in the plot would be to watch the house until none were left in it but the women and children.

Paul had scarcely turned where the road led to the house, when he saw a dark figure running through the shrubbery. He caught only a fleeting glimpse of the runner, but enough to show that he was going toward the house, and seeking to keep himself concealed. Hardly had he disappeared when Mendoza, Don José's overseer, came galloping up.

"Monsieur," he said, "I do not know who you are, but I crave your assistance. The levee has been cut, and unless the water can be stopped, the district will be flooded."

"Who is at the crevasse?" demanded Paul.

"Don José himself, with the Negroes."

"Can they hold it?"

"For a while, perhaps."

"Then come with me to the house," cried Paul, "for a greater danger threatens—fire, and worse."

As they rode forward, he rapidly explained the situation. Mendoza scowled fiercely, and with his right hand fingered the handle of the knife which rested in his belt.

"Ah," he remarked grimly, "they want revenge. Well, they shall have it, on the wrong side of their faces."

Rapidly they rode forward. The road by which they advanced was much longer than a direct line would have been, so much longer that when they came at length in sight of the plantation house they heard a medley of screams and wild shrieks and saw a flock of women scurrying out of the *patio*. A moment later a huge mulatto dashed from the house with a woman's limp form thrown across his shoulder, and simultaneously a thin column of smoke shot out from an open window.

The mulatto no sooner caught sight of the two white men than with a cry of rage he sprang into the shrubbery with his burden. Paul dared not fire at him for fear of striking Joséphine; and in the shrubbery a horse would be a useless incumbrance. He dismounted, followed by Mendoza. Simultaneously a cry of fire rang out.

"Damnation!" cried Mendoza. "I must save the house,

while you look after the señora. One white man is equal to ten Negroes."

Nevertheless, as Mendoza entered the house, the Negro desperado, standing behind the door, brained him with an ax. The overseer had lived by violence. He had made himself the instrument of the greed and avarice of others; he had done the dirty work of slavery, and had paid the price at the hands of one of the victims of the system. We never borrow but we must pay. Sooner or later the scales are balanced.

Paul followed the fleeing mulatto and his burden, and soon caught up with them. In spite of his huge strength, the man had wearied of the load. He stopped, and held the girl up before him, while with the other hand he drew a knife.

"Stop!" he said, "I'll parley."

Marchand stopped.

"Stand were you are until I have gone a hundred yards, and I'll drop the girl. Advance, and I'll cut her throat."

Here for the first time, in an emergency, Paul's quadroon training pushed itself to the front. The ordinary white man at such a juncture would have seen nothing but a white woman, in the grasp of a black brute. Paul Beaurepas—for the moment Paul Marchand—saw, beyond the evil countenance of the man who faced him, the long night of crime which had produced this fruit—the midnight foray in the forest, the slave coffle, the middle passage, the years of toil beneath the lash, the steady process of inbrutement which the careless endowment of white blood had intensified by just so much vigor and energy as the blood of the master had brought with it. He must save the woman, but he pitied, even while he condemned, the ravisher. Only a few weeks before, he himself had said, purely as a figure of speech, that if all the white race had but one neck, he could cheerfully wring it. To what extent could he blame this victim of a race's sins, who had suffered so much more, if he should seek to do to one of them what Paul Marchand had recently thought of as to all?

And this pity was very nearly his undoing. For while he paused, the second desperado, still bearing the bloody ax with which he had slain Mendoza, crept up behind him. Some instinct, or else some sudden change in the mulatto's expression, warned him in time to see the uplifted weapon, and, by a quick sidewise spring, learned in fencing, to avoid the blow. Ere the Negro could recover from his frustrated effort Marchand had drawn his sword and run him through.

The mulatto, seeing his scheme foiled, hesitated, lifted his knife over Joséphine's fair throat, and then with a lingering remnant of pity, threw her limp body to the ground and disappeared in the underbrush,—sure, wherever he went, to be so long as he lived the bane of the society which had produced him.

Marchand ran to the unconscious girl, and lifting her in his arms started toward the house, before reaching which he met Don José and one of his retainers.

"My daughter," cried Don José in anguished tones, "my daughter!"

"She has fainted, that is all. The scoundrel has done her no harm. He has escaped, but his companion is dead, out there in the bushes."

"And Mendoza?"

"Lies dead within the door, and the house is on fire. We must put it out."

Paul laid Joséphine upon the ground beneath a shady tree. One of the frightened Negro women came up, and took charge of her mistress, while Paul joined Morales in putting out the fire. Fortunately, the roof was fitted up with a tank, with a linen hose attached, which, strange to say, was in working order, and the fire, which had not gained much headway, was extinguished with no great difficulty.

When Joséphine had recovered consciousness, Señor Morales presented Paul, who had first taken time to remove some of the smoke from his face and hands.

"Joséphine," said her father, with a well-calculated expression of really sincere emotion, "behold your preserver—*our* preserver! To him you owe your honor and your life, and I Trois Pigeons!" Which was true in more senses than one. "In him behold the worthy son of our dear old friend and benefactor. He came to call upon us for friendship's sake, and so opportunely that there is nothing we would not do for him. Is it not so, Joséphine?"

Joséphine glanced shyly at her preserver. He was wonderfully like Philippe, but graver, and somewhat older. He did not look in the least like a quadroon.

"Monsieur is very good," she said politely, "and I am very grateful."

"Take her, my boy," said old Morales, embracing Paul with enthusiasm. "It was your father's wish and my promise; and more, she is yours by right of conquest. You have won her by the strength of your right arm."

At this moment Joséphine, for whom events were moving too rapidly, created a diversion by a sharp exclamation of pain, and at the same moment a servant ran up to say that the levee was safe, so Marchand was not compelled to reply. He remained at Trois Pigeons for several hours, however, until Joséphine had been put to bed for her nerves, and Mendoza's body had been decently laid out for interment, after which he rode slowly and thoughtfully back to the city. Joséphine was very beautiful. A month before he would scarcely have dared look at her. Today he had held her in his arms. It was not a case where distance lent enchantment, for this close proximity but enhanced her charm. It would have been next to impossible for a Creole gentleman under thirty, to hold Joséphine Morales in his arms for two minutes without being powerfully moved.

They buried Mendoza on a little hillock that rose in the field. The Negroes never went near the place except in groups, and it was said among them, with bated breath, that the overseer's ghost, with gory head cleft in twain, and carrying his heavy rawhide slave whip, still haunted the canebrake, looking for stray Negroes upon whom to wreak revenge for his own undoing.

XVII.

Paul's Dilemma

The impassivity which had characterized Paul Beaurepas's demeanor since his new birth had masked a seething caldron of emotions, and had been achieved by very great effort. No more radical change in one's life would have been possible. In one moment, by the stroke of a decrepit old man's pen, he was raised from a man of color to a white man. What that might mean in the South today is at least conceivable to any thoughtful, observant person who reads the newspapers. The reader must have already gathered something of what it meant in New Orleans in 1820, but to make it entirely clear a little further explanation may not be amiss, even at the expense of some repetition, because any merit which this story may have as a social study must depend upon a reasonably accurate knowledge of the conditions which surrounded those who figure in it.

Under the old regime the *gens de couleur* or colored people of Louisiana, were a separate class, inferior to the whites, but superior in the eyes of the whites and vastly more so in their own eyes, to the Negroes, who were not only black but mostly slaves as well, while the people of color were in large part free. The term "Negro" was never applied to them directly except by way of insult. The term "colored" meant, in common parlance, as now in Latin-America, and elsewhere than in the United States, of mixed blood.

Among themselves distinctions of color were jealously guarded, the quadroon or three-quarters white outranking the mulatto, the octoroon or seven-eighths white taking precedence of the quadroon. The term "quadroon," however, was generically employed to distinguish the class or caste.

Men of color, like the pseudo Paul Marchand, were often men of affairs and of means, merchants, landlords and planters. Some of them like Marchand, were educated in France, where they sent their children to be taught. Some of them remained in Europe, and some returned to Louisiana. Like the white Creoles, they had had a strong feeling of local attachment. They were denied civil and social equality, including the right of intermarriage, and they were not admitted to the professions, but beyond these limits the amenities were as a general thing fairly well observed when the men of the races met for business or otherwise.

The women of color were in a more precarious position. Many of them, moved by a perverted social ambition for themselves or for their children, preferred to be white men's mistresses rather than marry men darker than themselves or even of their own degree of color. When their children became white enough it was not hard to cross the line and pass for white. Many of the quadroon women, however, secured the same result, for themselves and for their children, by attaining honorable marriage and moving to France, where there were no social distinctions based on color.

The lot of the free quadroons, therefore, might seem to have been enviable, compared with that of the black slaves. But the very privileges they enjoyed, and the refinement of feeling that grew out of them, only made them more keenly alive to the things they were denied. Under the older French regime this had not been so noticeable; the Latin affinity for darker races, the Latin gaiety, had softened the lines of caste, had permitted much kindliness of feeling among masters and slaves, and had recognized the ties of kinship among the mixed people. But the advent of the more northern American had changed all this. Bringing with him an exaggerated scorn of dark blood, his ideas had quickly given color to the public thought.

In this transition period, the quadroon felt the pressure most keenly. To the slave these changes meant little. At the lowest stage of human fortune, he could sink no deeper; he had reached the bed-rock of degradation, so far as he or any one else could see. Having never had any privileges, he had none to lose. To the quadroon, every old right denied, every former privilege withheld, was but pushing him back deeper into the mire. For instance, the free colored battalion had rendered gallant service in the War of 1812. Its disbandment, in deference to the growing sentiment that to bear arms was the prerogative of white men only, was a bitter blow to the quadroon pride. In earlier days certain boxes in the Opera House were open to the quadroons. Their relegation to the gallery, with the Negroes, had been a keener blow than the denial of the suffrage or the right to serve on jury had ever seemed. A man might vote but once a year; it was the little daily slights that stung.

Among the more thoughtful of them, when they came together, the conversation turned always, sooner or later, on the melancholy theme of their wrongs. The ever-present grievance tinctured every thought. The great currents of life, the movement of nations, the advancement of science, the development of art, already dwarfed by distance from great cities, were as nothing to the question of whether a quadroon could eat at a restaurant, attend the theater, or take precedence, in colored society, of a mulatto or man of a lesser degree of white blood.

Some of the quadroons found comfort in a semi-tropical lethargy; others in the debauchery to which in part they owed their origin. Some managed to hold up their own heads by looking down upon those beneath them.

Into this unnatural and painful position Paul Marchand's lot had been cast. In youth it had not been so bad. There was music and love and the hope that springs eternal in the heart of youth. During the few years he had spent in Paris, he had well nigh forgotten that he was anything less than a man.

For a time he had dreamed, over there in France, that he might return to New Orleans and preach the doctrine of human equality; not offensively, but persuasively, appealing to men's reason and their sense of justice. He soon learned that this was impracticable, if not impossible, and that the condition of his own existence was that he should accept the established order and be content with the place assigned to men like him.

The lesson had not been easily learned. His self-respect had clamored for its life. When confronted by the inevitable, he had, for a time, taken refuge in the weaker position, that by force of the preponderance of his white blood, he ought to be a white man; that it was an outrage that the undistinguishable drop of black blood which lurked somewhere beneath his skin, should degrade him to the position of a man of color.

He might have passed for white. The city had grown so rapidly during his absence that upon his return from Europe he could, with a little friendly reticence on the part of his acquaintance, have easily lost his identity and established a new one. But this chance he had forfeited by marrying a quadroon woman and thus accepting the ban of caste. His wife had brought him wealth. Nevertheless, such is the perversity of the human heart, that he was not entirely satisfied with the bargain. He loved his wife and would have kept her in all honor and respect, and her patrimony had placed him in the ranks of the financially well-to-do, and yet he would have exercised the rights and enjoyed the privileges of a white man. The effort to transmute this mental attitude into concrete action had landed Paul Marchand in the Calabozo, from which his father's death had opportunely released him.

But now all this was changed. As by magic, the door hopelessly sealed had opened and he had been drawn in. The pauper in the world's best things had become the prince who could command them all—great wealth, high social position, unlimited opportunity. Moreover, he was free to marry again, for, by the law of Louisiana, the marriage of a white person to a person of color was null and void. By the stern rule which placed race above every other consideration, a man might father his own slaves, and sell the unfortunate fruit of his loins in the market. He might increase the quadroon caste to any limit, but without the sanction of church or state, nor did either church or state do aught to prevent it. By a legal fiction, which grew into a habit of thought that was to last for generations to come, a man was black for all social purposes, so long as he acknowledged or was known to carry in his veins a drop of black blood. By his accession to the white race Paul Beaurepas, formerly Marchand, f.m.c. became, *ipso facto*, an unmarried man, and by virtue of his wealth and position as the head of a great family, an eligible aspirant for the hand of any unmarried white woman in Louisiana.

And Julie, and her children? If he so chose, they must accept the inevitable. Julie's birth had not been wrapped in mystery nor had her life been colored by romance, except that of Paul's love. Her parentage was well known, and she bore upon her shapely features, in the warmth of her tint and the wave of her hair, the faint though quite distinguishable imprint of her mother's race. No matter how sweet or desirable she might be as a woman, no fairy tale could make her white, nor could she be a white man's lawful wife in Louisiana.

And Julie's children? Curiously enough, Marchand found himself thinking of them as *her* children. A week before, they had been *his* children. He had not only loved them, but had been proud of them—now he could only be ashamed of them. They belonged in the category of surreptitious things, not to be spoken of, except perhaps among boon companions, in the mellow house when wine had unsealed the lips, and men were merely men and good fellows.

To say that Paul was not strongly tempted, would be untrue. The beauty of Joséphine Morales was the topic of New Orleans. A dozen of the young bloods of the city would cheerfully have fought for her, given the opportunity; but Philippe Beaurepas was the only one who had more than a speaking or dancing acquaintance with her, and her fate had been fixed almost from her birth. She was the price of Trois Pigeons, and no man not able to lift its mortgage might dare raise his eyes to her. This was no delicately veiled family understanding, such as might exist among a colder and more hypocritical people. With her father's pride of blood and her own dower of beauty, Joséphine was frankly in the market, for sale to the highest bidder. Philippe had been the favorite, by reason of his expectations. With Philippe out of the way, the field was open to another. Provided he were rich enough and of good family, neither youth nor beauty mattered on his part, nor tears nor regrets on Joséphine's. As race was above mere vulgar justice or humanity, so pride of blood and possessions were above any so inconsiderable a thing as love.

To Paul Beaurepas, then, this beauty had been offered—thrown at his head, so to speak. For old Morales was not troubled by fine distinctions of sentiment. The man was white, he was of good blood; his financial position was unassailable, and he held a mortgage on Trois Pigeons for more than the plantation was worth. It was inconceivable that one brought up as Paul had been, to whom white women had been taboo, should fail to appreciate or even to exaggerate the worth of Joséphine's hitherto forbidden charms.

But to Paul Julie was the fly in the ointment. To leave her, to give back the wealth he had received with her, now a mere pittance beside his princely inheritance, would, he feared, break her heart; and he loved her too well to wish to hurt her. That she would be content to live under his protection, and see another woman claim him as husband, he did not believe; nor would he have cared to lead a double life, however easy a lax code of morals might make it, nor could he have respected a wife who would condone such a course. It was one or the other; he must choose between the two. If he married Joséphine, he must definitely renounce Julie. If he gave up the thought of marriage with any other woman, Julie might perhaps be satisfied to count their marriage as good in spite of the law, and to bear, for love of him, the odium which attached to an unlegalized connection.

While he wrestled with his problem, during the two weeks which had elapsed since the reading of the will, he had not slept at home, spending his days at his office and his nights at the house he had inherited, where old Terence, retained upon wages, waited upon him and gave him an insight into his late master's affairs. He had written several times to Julie, brief notes, to say that he was busy, and that he would be for a few days at his father's house, and that she must not worry about his absence.

XVIII.

The Decision

A week after the duel, Paul Beaurepas sent each of his cousins, by old Terence, a written invitation to dine at the family mansion on Royal Street. Their physical wounds were sufficiently healed to permit their attendance, though Raoul bore a scar upon his cheek, Hector wore a bit of plaster on his ear, and Henri walked with a cane. Their spirits, however, were still sore, and had they dared, they would have declined the invitation. With the exception of Philippe, despite their outward mask of deference, not one of them but hated the interloper with a sullen fury, all the more venomous because futile. But the invitation had all the force of a command. Paul Beaurepas was their creditor. He had intimated in his letter that this interview would fix the relations which should exist in the future between him and his new-found cousins, to whom it was of prime importance that these relations should be friendly.

The beautiful dining-room, decorated in the style of Louis Quinze, with mirrors between the tall windows, and figures around the ceiling, molded in stucco, lighted by a vast chandelier filled with wax candles, had been freshly renovated for the occasion. There were bunches of roses on the table, which was set with the family plate, in part inherited, and in part imported by old Pierre at the time of his marriage many years before. The menu exhausted the art of the Creole kitchen, which was famous for culinary excellence, and was served by old Terence, assisted by a deft-handed, light-footed mulatto boy.

There was at the beginning a certain air of constraint among the cousins, which Paul did his best to lighten. They had been surprised and humiliated by the result of the meeting at the Oaks, and were wondering whether their kinsmen might not have some further fantastic scheme of revenge to spring upon them. Since the meeting, they no longer had any doubts—if they had ever had any based on anything but self-interest—about the descent and racial purity of the *ci-devant* quadroon. He had proved his blood by his deeds—and they liked to think that any one of them could have done the same thing in his place. It was worthy of a Beaurepas.

But they were manifestly uneasy. Philippe was perhaps the least disturbed. His participation in the duel had been indeed "a mere formality," he having given his cousin no cause of offense; and in such of the family conferences as had taken place since then, he had played, so far as loyalty to his brother and his other cousins would permit, the part of a peace-maker. They would gain nothing, he argued, by a bellicose attitude. They were absolutely at their cousin Paul's mercy. It would be impossible to break the will, and, if they spoke their new found kinsman fair, he might deal leniently, perhaps, even generously, with them.

For, when all was said, he was a Beaurepas, and the pride of family which he had already displayed would no doubt stretch to include his cousins. He had been given the satisfaction of a gentleman for his fancied insults. He was the head of the family, and one cannot be a head without a following. In business, in public life, should he choose to enter it, and especially on the new social sea upon which he must now seek to float, the good-will of his five cousins could not but be of value. It was true that he could crush them, but would it be wise or prudent to do so? Bankrupt, discredited, they would be worth nothing to him. But so long as they could hold up their heads, they were still in the forefront of Creole society. They could put him up at clubs and introduce him to the best people, and in politics their clan support would be an important asset.

As the meal progressed, however, and the wine went round, some of the constraint wore off. The guests told stories of social happenings, which they supposed might, from their novelty to him, be of interest to their host. They detailed the more or less scandalous gossip of the clubs and gaming houses, and the rumors of the cotton market and the stock exchange. They discussed the French company which was playing in repertory at the New Orleans Theater. The opera and the quadroon ball were not mentioned—it was excellent policy to let sleeping dogs lie.

When the coffee had been served and Terence had decanted and set before them several bottles of the vintage Burgundy which old Pierre had imported twenty years before, Paul Marchand's face grew grave, he seemed preoccupied, and an air of anxious expectation settled upon the faces of his guests. Finally the host rose and spoke.

"Gentlemen and cousins," he said, "in pursuance of the suggestion conveyed to you in my letter, I have summoned you here tonight with a twofold purpose—first, to return, as well as I may, your courtesy and hospitality so cordially tendered me upon my accession to my inheritance, and, secondly, to make a fitting response to your offer of friendship and fealty. The first you may consider done; I am proud to welcome you, as host, to a table where you were at home before I was, and I appreciate to the full what must seem to you the hard fate which gives to me what any one of you might well have anticipated as his own."

"I find myself in a unique and difficult position—one absolutely novel, so far as I can learn, in the history of Louisiana. Doubtless there have been unfortunate white children whose parents have abandoned them to nameless obscurity. But never before, I like to think, has the legitimate son of a good family been condemned by his parents to an inferior class solely to gratify a woman's selfish pride and a man's sentimental weakness—if not callous indifference—and then, after many years, been recalled to his own race and family."

"I need not dwell upon the moral and spiritual aspects of a quadroon's life. A little imagination, it seems to me, ought to make them vivid enough. They are too painful to dwell upon, but such as they are, I suffered them."

"While doing so, I condemned the laws and customs which degraded me, and would have changed them if I could. Nor have I altered my views. A man whose opinions upon a vital subject differ from those of the majority, and who would not play the part of a coward by denying or concealing or living counter to his convictions, could not live usefully or happily, if he could live at all, in Louisiana. Some day these laws will pass, these customs change—I hope the change will not come, as it did in France or in the island across the Gulf, in a deluge of blood, but come it will, if not in our time, then in that of our children. Could I by remaining here advance that day, I would do so gladly."

Does he mean, thought the cousins, to sell out and move away, taking with him our chief claim to financial credit and social distinction, the family fortune, and all for a mawkish negrophile sentiment? It would be a base, a dastardly thing to do!

"And I have still another embarrassment," Paul went on. "Under the former misconception as to my condition, I married a free woman of color. She brought me the larger freedom which wealth brings in some degree to even a quadroon. She has made me a faithful and devoted wife and has borne me two bright and beautiful children. What is her position under the laws of Louisiana? While I was supposedly a quadroon, she was an honored wife, they were legitimate children, if only those of a man of color; now she is nothing—a light woman, a *milatresse*, and they are simply a gentleman's byblows."

"I have spoken, as you have spoken, of the honor of the Beaurepas. Is it honor to forswear a solemn obligation, assumed with the sanction of God and man?—for these our marriage had until a few weeks since. Is it honorable to abandon one's children to a nameless and hopeless future, as my parents so long abandoned me? Would it be honorable to keep them in any other relationship than that of honest and open family life? To me it would seem the depth of dishonor. I must confess, gentlemen, that my father's experiment has proved a failure."

"My cousin Henri once said, quite truthfully, in my hearing, though the remark was not addressed to me, that blood without breeding cannot make a gentleman. It may be said with equal truth that the race consciousness which is the strongest of the Creole characteristics, is not a matter of blood alone, but in large part the product of education and environment; it is social rather than personal. A man cannot, at my age, change easily his whole outlook upon life, nor can one trained as a quadroon become over night a—Beaurepas.

In New Orleans, where a man must be of one caste or another, where there is no place for the individual as such, I, who have been all my life without father or mother, now find myself, in sympathy, without a race. In other words, gentlemen, M. Pierre Beaurepas has bequeathed me a pair of seven-league boots which do not fit, and which I cannot wear. It is the culminating tragedy of my life thus far that I can find no pleasure in the headship of this fine old family, with all its opportunities for development and usefulness, and I can feel no spark of filial love or tenderness for a father whom I never knew, and a mother who repented of and dreaded my existence."

"What then, gentlemen? Fortunately there is a way out, which more than one white man of New Orleans has taken before, as well as some of our quadroon kinsmen. In a very short time I shall leave New Orleans and move with my family to France, where men are judged by their worth and not by their color, where in all honor my wife can be my wife and my children my children and I need not be ashamed of them nor they afraid of me."

His voice had been affected by emotion, and while he lifted his glass to moisten his lips, the cousins regarded one another dolefully. Their worst fears were realized. Gone would soon be the wealth and prestige of the family, and they would be left mere ordinary Creoles, of mediocre parts and financially on the rocks! But their cousin had not finished.

"Certain notes were given by you gentlemen to your late uncle," he went on, "for money loaned, and have come to me as part of the inheritance. They have, I think, served their purpose. They were intended, I believe, to deceive, and had that effect—they were given as suggested advancements, and received in that light. They were meant to place you in my power and have done so; but as I am in no danger from you, and have no designs against you, and only wish you well, I take pleasure in returning them to you."

"That is generous of you, cousin," said Henri.

"Yes," added Raoul, "we thank you very much."

"The slaves belonging to the estate I shall manumit—that much of my prerogative as heir I shall exercise. I wish I could wipe out the system as easily—I consider it the sum of all villainies. The remainder of the property, in its entirety, I shall relinquish. I cannot hold it upon the conditions, expressed or implied, which M. Pierre Beaurepas has made, nor could I in honor keep it otherwise."

The faces of the cousins reflected the joy to which this statement gave quick rise. If their cousin should renounce the inheritance, it would come to them by law, as their uncle's next of kin, in equal shares. One-fifth of the estate would be a fortune for each. But this spark of hope was rudely extinguished, for all but one of them, by the speaker's next words.

"I shall transfer it, by proper legal conveyance," he continued, "to M. Philippe Beaurepas, whom I have chosen as my successor, with the confident hope that he will use it for the honor and glory of a family which means so much to him and to you all and to Louisiana, but which, I say it sadly, can mean nothing to me. The honor that I fought you for the other day, was not the honor of the family; it was my own starved honor, my own maimed self-respect which clamored for satisfaction. I shall not even assume the family name—I would not bear the name of a man who would treat his son as M. Pierre Beaurepas has treated me."

It was apparent that the iron had entered Paul Beaurepas's soul very deeply. The cousins recalled, later on, when they were talking over this meeting,—as Don José Morales had observed upon a previous occasion,—that rarely had

Paul referred to their uncle as his father. Before any one could speak Paul Beaurepas resumed:

"And now, gentlemen, I give you the health of M. Philippe Beaurepas, your cousin, *our* cousin, the heir of the estate and the head of the family."

They were so dazed by their host's announcement that they drank the toast in silence. Presently Philippe, having recovered somewhat from his amazement, rose to his feet.

"Cousin," he said, his voice faltering with emotion, "you have taken us all by surprise—me most of all. You have been shabbily treated, and you have taken a generous revenge. Despite your disclaimer, you have maintained the honor of the family upon the loftiest plane. I know no other man who would be capable of what you are about to do—I know that I should not. Words are inadequate, even could I command them, to express my gratitude. I can only say that I shall try to wear my honors worthily, and shall regard the property as a trust to be administered in a manner that will conform to my uncle's wishes and meet with your approval and be a credit to the family and to humanity. And I shall, as no doubt you would wish, extend to my brother and my other cousins all proper kinsmanly devotion. You have opened to me, cousin, by your munificence, a future which is all bright. And I wish you and yours, in your distant home, all the happiness which you have placed it in my power to achieve for myself and another who is dear to me."

"Among the assets I shall turn over to you, dear cousin," resumed Paul, with a tender smile,—was it tinged with regret?—"is the mortgage on Trois Pigeons, on the condition that you settle it in the manner your uncle intended."

"It is the greatest gift of all," returned Philippe, gratefully. "I think my uncle meant her for a better man, but I will take her and be thankful. I have loved her all her life."

Paul had meant to terminate the interview at this point. He had made his great renunciation and touched the dramatic climax of the play. He had dealt, he thought, generously with his kinsmen. Philippe had spoken from the heart. The others had thanked him with their lips, but he could read from their faces that, freed from the menace of their outstanding debts and with nothing further to hope for, they frankly hated him for his preference of Philippe, and Philippe because he had been preferred. So he hardened his heart and shot his last bolt,—it would strike Philippe as well, but he must take the bitter with the sweet—the others must not escape.

"I have one thing more to say," said Paul. "It concerns a matter involving, radically, the standing of the family. I have hesitated to speak of it, but I think, as representatives of a proud house and a proud race, you ought to know it. In looking though the late M. Pierre Beaurepas's papers, I discovered incontestable proof that of the five children who were brought to New Orleans from San Domingo, one, though also a cousin, was of quadroon birth. The five children who came from San Domingo grew up into you five gentlemen. The corollary is obvious."

"I thought it no more than your right to know this. And whether you shall learn any more, I leave to you. It had occurred to me that you might desire, for the sake of racial purity and the family honor, to expel this cuckoo from the nest, this intruder from your midst; that you might not wish longer to meet on terms of kinship and equality this baseborn interloper, who—through no fault of his own, it is true, and in all ignorance, but none the less unlawfully,—is exercising the rights and privileges of a well-born white man. Since I am going away and have no longer any direct personal interest, I feel no responsibility in the matter. Gentlemen, I leave it to you whether I shall name the man. Shall I or shall I not?"

The cousins were dazed, if possible, more completely than before. They had supposed their capacity for astonishment exhausted, but this announcement had sounded new depths. They looked at one another furtively, and studied their own reflections in the mirrors which lined the walls of the dining-room. One perceived in another a certain breadth of nostril, but in himself a certain fulness of lip—in one a certain thickness of eyelid, in himself a certain wave of the hair. They examined their fingernails furtively for the telltale black streak. For a moment no one spoke.

"Which shall it be, gentlemen?" asked Paul softly, "yes or no?"

The answer came as one voice.

"No!"

"I think you have chosen wisely," said Paul, suavely, "and I assure you that the secret shall remain locked inviolably in my own bosom."

There was a happy woman in the house on Bourbon Street a little later in the evening. Julie's fears were dissipated, an honorable future for herself and her children assured.

In another land, where kindlier customs prevailed, Paul Marchand prospered in business, and reared a family of sons and daughters, some of whom distinguished themselves in various walks of life. A son, a lieutenant in the French Navy, came to the United States in 1863. He was attached, as an observation officer, to Admiral Farragut's staff, and was present at the taking of the city of New Orleans. Philippe Beaurepas, then past middle life, and later one of the first of the reconstructed rebels, entertained him at dinner in the old house on Royal Street, where he still lived, though in diminished state, for while the honor of the family proved safe in Philippe's hands, he was not a good business man and the family fortune had sadly dwindled. He had married Joséphine Morales, and their union had proved a happy one. They lived in the family mansion and kept Trois Pigeons as a country place. They named their first son Paul.

It might be supposed that the fact disclosed to Paul's cousins at the second dinner, as to the origin of some one of them, would have made them more tolerant of those of darker blood. But, with the exception of Philippe, it had the contrary effect. Henri was killed in a duel, Adolphe died of yellow fever, but the survivors and their descendants, some of whom achieved prominence in public life, were ever in the forefront of any agitation to limit the rights or restrict the privileges of their darker fellow citizens. They helped procure the passage of a law forbidding the manumission of slaves, and led an abortive movement to expel all free colored people from Louisiana. They fought gallantly for slavery in the Civil War, were leaders and advisers of the Ku-Klux-Klan, and prominent in the "redemption" of Louisiana and the nullification of the Fifteenth Amendment. A grandson of Henri Beaurepas not long since introduced in the Louisiana legislature an amendment to the criminal code, making marriage a felony between a white person and a person of colored blood to the thirty-second degree inclusive. One wonders if he had ever learned of the ancestral possibility.

The End.